HUNTED

ALIAS #2

____

LISA HUGHEY

Acknowledgments

As always, thanks to Deb Nemeth for her awesome editing and her patience for my mistakes (many and varied). I'm always learning and growing with her editorial input.

Thanks to Robin Ludwig at www.gobookcoverdesign.com for her amazing cover!!

So thankful for the many writer friends who continue to be a source of support and inspiration. Adrienne, Lynn, Rachael, Sophie, Cecilia, Mysti, Vanessa, Shannon, Gigi, Julie.

Shout out to Adrienne Bell for the read throughs and suggestions.

To my husband for his unwavering support.

Chapter One

L ife couldn't get any better.

Tupua "Dwayne" Lameko sauntered toward his boss's office, whistling contentedly. Last night had been just what he needed. He was relaxed, sexually sated, and full of good humor. Anticipation fizzed through him. Jillian Larsen, cofounder of Adams-Larsen Inc. and Associates—or ALIAS, as the employees liked to call it—had called him in early this morning, and he was hoping for an exciting new assignment.

He was anxious for heart-pumping action.

Maybe something with physical protection where he got to use his body. But whatever he did, he'd be in the field and away from—

"Oh." He stopped, nearly stumbled.

Behind the receptionist's desk outside Jillian's office sat Maria Torres. The woman he needed to get some distance from.

For some bizarre reason, she turned him into a bumbling, unconfident rube. "Uh, you're here early." *Smooth, Lameko.*

Maria flushed and ducked her head.

Dwayne took a step back, trying not to crowd her. She'd been through enough and he sure as hell didn't want to scare the poor woman.

Her silky ebony hair shone in the low office light. Her fingers tightened on the folder she held in front of her like a shield.

Dammit. He had scared her. "Jill here?"

"Go on in." Her soft tones were barely audible even though there was an expectant hush in the office. "She's waiting for you."

Dwayne hustled into Jill's office and let out a stressed sigh. Why did that woman, who should be the least threatening woman on the planet, rattle him?

Before he closed the door, he shot a final glance at Maria. Her head was bent while she stared at her desktop.

The vulnerable nape of her neck was scattered with fine hairs—appearing soft, but certainly not weak. She had kicked major ass. Every time he came face to face with her deep burled mahogany eyes, rounded cheeks, lush plump lips, and full-figured curves, his immediate, completely inappropriate, thought was she would be a lusty armful.

And that's why he was going to hell.

Because he was inconveniently, ill-advisedly, out-of-his-freaking-mind, attracted to her.

Her overblown figure and slumberous eyes tripped his trigger in a major way. But what really did it for him?

Her spirit, her sheer *bolos*, to triumph over insurmountable odds, to move across the country to live in a city where she knew one person, Jill, was the cherry on top of her gorgeous forbidden sundae.

Lately he'd taken to one-night stands—a fact his mama

was not happy about—just to try and fuck away his attraction to the off-limits Maria Torres.

She'd begun to come out of her shell, and her personality was as attractive as her physicality. Except when he was around. Then she was skittish, on the shy side, and definitely uncomfortable. He hated that she was afraid of him.

So even though he was crazy attracted to her, there was no way in hell anything was happening between them. He'd been cordial ever since she'd come to work at the office. But he knew he scared her and that was not acceptable.

"Dwayne," Jill said brusquely.

He blinked, came back to awareness.

"Good to see you." Jillian Larsen was Maria Torres's polar opposite. Slender, platinum blonde, fair skin and slate-gray eyes, always clad in neutral tailored suits that were subtly sexy. She and her friend Marsh Adams had teamed up to start Adams-Larsen, a private witness protection firm. Every day Dwayne was thankful for this job, where he was making a difference.

"Morning." He nodded.

"We have a situation."

MARIA TORRES BLEW out an annoyed breath.

Dwayne—the player—Lameko always seemed one step away from bolting whenever he came into her sphere. As if *she* were the spider rather than the fly caught in his sexual web.

Ha.

She wanted him. Bad. But she had no idea how to go about getting him. The guy who had no compunction about picking up a woman for the night—assuming the office rumors were true—would not even come close to her. He seemed to go out of his way to flee *from* her.

Her shoulders slumped.

Maybe that in and of itself was telling. He didn't want the damaged freak.

Her friends in California would say, "Go after him, girl."

She'd escaped a morally bankrupt politician who had held her hostage in solitary confinement for more than eight years, but some days she wondered if she'd used up all her bravado planning and executing her escape from her prison.

She was afraid.

She didn't want to be afraid, but she couldn't seem to stop.

Her default was either scared or angry, except around Dwayne, when she became inept at forming words. Her heart banged against her ribcage and crowded her throat until she could only mumble in his presence.

And since that attraction was a dead end, she needed to focus on her life and what she was going to do next. The problem was…she had no idea. But it was time to consider her future.

When he closed the door to Jill's office, she relaxed.

The front doorbell buzzed.

Maria peered at the security monitor, wondering who was here this early. Probably the client Jill and Dwayne were waiting for. She depressed the intercom button. "Hello."

The girl at the door jumped about a foot in the air, then twisted her head back and forth, searching for a hidden enemy, her terror plain to see.

"Camera up and to your right."

The stick-thin girl in a luxurious wool coat wrapped her arms around her waist protectively. She peered at the camera from underneath the matching knit cap that hid most of her face, revealing thick long eyelashes that glimmered with tears. She seemed to shake off her fear and pressed the intercom button. "I'm here to see Jillian Larsen."

"Name?"

"I'd rather not say." She glanced around furtively.

"Are we expecting you?"

"Sort of."

"One moment."

Fear rolled off the woman. Nausea swirled in the pit of Maria's stomach. Her first impulse was to let her inside but she followed protocol and confirmed with Jill that the woman-girl scared of her own shadow did, in fact, have an appointment. Maria hustled down the stairs and opened the front door.

The girl threw herself inside the restored old brownstone and slammed her back against the closed door. One hand over her heart, she closed her eyes, the thick fan of her caramel lashes dark against her bleached white cheeks, her chest heaving. "Sorry, sorry."

It wasn't Maria's place to judge, so she put away her concern and the glimmer of anxiety that transmitted from the woman and into her. The girl was stunning—gorgeous smooth cream skin, perfectly shaped eyebrows, hair a multitude of shades from auburn to caramel to a honey blond, and aristocratic cheekbones dusted pink. Her lips were a glossy cotton-candy pink that matched the bits of color in her bouclé wool coat.

The girl with no name was so shiny and perfect that she didn't seem real. Except for the fear.

The girl shook off her insecurity and regained her composure before Maria's eyes. Her shoulders relaxed, her chin elevated, and her mouth curved into a plastic, impersonal smile. "Well now that I'm inside—Elizabeth Vandenbeek—but call me Bitsy."

Bitsy?

She extended her elegant, bony fingers and Maria clasped her hand with reluctance.

Maria was…solid. Not fat, but not ultrathin like this woman, and her pudgy fingers felt large in the woman's grasp.

But if she'd been a delicate flower, she'd have never made it out of her prison. So, yeah. There was that.

Maria pulled her hand away, still uncomfortable with being touched.

"You seem familiar." Bitsy squinted at Maria as if trying to place her.

Hopefully she didn't follow politics or the crime pages.

"I don't believe we've met." Which of course they hadn't, because for all her progress, Maria mostly went from the office to her studio apartment, and back again. The irrational panicky fear that hit her at odd times restricted her movements as easily as if she were tethered by an actual ball and chain. Maria turned to lead her to the office upstairs. "Jillian's office is this way."

Bitsy followed Maria up the grand staircase to Jill's office. Her boss was her savior, her role model, and her confidante all in one.

Maria headed to the closed door, but after she knocked, Bitsy gasped.

"What's wrong?" Maria whirled, her fight-or-flight response kicking into high gear. She put the girl behind her and searched for the threat.

"It's you."

She was what was wrong? Maria didn't follow.

"I mean, you're her."

All the fight went out of her. Oh, that. She guessed it was too much to hope that Bitsy didn't follow the news. Even though she'd tried to stay out of the limelight, some pictures of her had made it into the media during the trial.

"Everyone was talking about you. About how brave you are." The girl grabbed Maria, her clasp surprisingly strong for such delicate bones. "Were you terrified?"

Maria's hands went clammy, shook. She didn't want to annoy the client, but she hated to be touched without warning.

Her stomach revolted but she clamped down and smiled tightly.

She didn't talk about what happened to her.

She'd been offered a lot of money to tell the world about her ordeal. About the sheer terror of her abduction and then her horrified disbelief when they'd taken away the other girls and left her to rot in that underground cell.

About how her hope had slowly withered and died, just like the crops in the fields after the harvest. The crushing sense of loss in her heart when she finally accepted that no one was coming for her.

But it was private, personal. However that didn't stop the media and the public from speculating about her.

Bitsy gripped Maria's arm tightly. "You know how scary this is."

Maria wanted to rip the girl's fingers from her arm. Instead she gently removed the girl's hand. "I'll let Jillian know you're here."

Curiosity sparked as she wondered what this naïve young girl was doing at Adams-Larsen. But that didn't matter. Bitsy Vandenbeek had nothing to do with her.

The girl reached for her again. Maria shoved Bitsy into

the occupied office, for once so rattled that she didn't have time to stutter around Dwayne.

"Bitsy Vandenbeek to see you." Then Maria shut the door.

She sank into the chair behind her receptionist desk. Would the unrelenting fear, the aversion to physical contact, and the rage that seemed to explode with no warning *ever* go away?

Now that the girl was in Jill's office and she was done dealing with Ms. Vandenbeek, Maria could breathe.

The intercom buzzed. "Maria. We're going to need you."

Chapter Two

Dwayne had caught Maria's rattled gaze before she shut the door.

The instinct to soothe her burned like a fire in his heart. He even took a step toward the exit before he stopped. What the hell was that about?

Jillian snagged his attention and introduced him to Bitsy Vandenbeek.

"Hello." He spared their guest a quick glance before craning his neck and waiting for Maria to come back, so he could confirm she was okay.

"Have a seat." Jill gestured to the casual grouping of wing chairs and settee, even though Bitsy looked like she belonged in the lineup for a debutante ball and would be more at home in the formal office section with the massive partner's desk and chairs. Some days he couldn't believe he knew what a freaking debutante ball was. That was how much his life had changed since he'd ventured beyond his family-centric Samoan community and embraced the world of law enforcement and saving people.

The office door opened, and Maria came in with a notebook and pen.

Dwayne searched Maria's features, but she'd perfected that blank face and blocked her thoughts and emotions from him. From everyone. He'd seen it happen before, but today he wanted to smash through that barricade and ask what was wrong.

She was already afraid of him. No reason to make it worse, so he let it go.

She clutched the steno pad in white fingers, her head bent, hiding from the rest of the room.

Dwayne sank into the seat next to Jill while Maria tried to blend into the wallpaper.

Bitsy perched on the edge of the robin's-egg blue settee, looking for all the world like she was one step away from bolting. Her hands fluttered reminding him of the hummingbirds that stuck their noses into his mother's flowers to soak up all the nectar. She didn't sit still, her movements filled with agitation.

"Tell us about your problem."

Bitsy proceeded to describe in concise detail why she needed ALIAS's services. And holy shit, did she.

Her stepfather, the powerful, well-connected CEO of a pharmaceutical company, had his mistress killed. The woman's death was ruled a random act of violence, but Bitsy overheard her stepfather confirming the details of her "random" death.

Her stepfather was old money, a member of the "less government is better, in order preserve his own fortune" kind of guy. Van Pharmaceuticals was under fire for raising the price of several lifesaving drugs. But they used a powerful spin firm to convince the public that the price increases were needed to keep making the necessary drugs.

His girlfriend had been the main lobbyist for Van Pharmaceuticals when she was killed in a mugging while running in Rock Creek Park. The smear in the press had been easy to accomplish. She should never have been running alone in the park in a pair of small spandex shorts and revealing sports bra.

While her murder was unsolved, the general consensus had been to warn women about running alone and place the blame square on the woman for not following safety precautions.

Except Bitsy had heard her stepfather talking with his head of security, Louis Gerber. Based on her recitation of the convo, her stepfather had conspired to kill his girlfriend before she exposed the illegal contributions and bribes her K Street lobbying firm had paid to senators in order to shut down the senate investigation into the drug company corruption. They hadn't succeeded and the hearing on the prescription drug price increases was due to start next week.

Dwayne perked up.

When he'd worked for the FBI, he'd been in the white-collar crime division. That must be why Jill tagged him for this meeting.

Dwayne observed while Jillian asked the questions. "Why don't you go to the authorities?"

Bitsy twisted her fingers together. "No one will believe me."

It would be a hard sell, and skeptics might believe Bitsy invented the whole thing.

Dwayne split his attention between the bird and Maria, noting her micro reactions to the girl's tale. She held her body stiff, scratching notes on the pad intermittently, like she wasn't writing down anything pertinent. But she was listening, absorbing.

Jill placed her hand on Bitsy's wrist. The girl had refused to take her coat off. By now she must be baking as the heating system had dispelled the early morning chill from the old brownstone and the office was toasty.

"What about leaking the information to journalists?" Dwayne pressed.

His sister, Samaria, would salivate for a scoop like that. She'd been freelancing while looking for a full-time job with a news outlet. Bitsy should have contacts through her job as a columnist for the Post.

"I didn't want to put my mother through the strain of having to deal with the press."

"Bitsy." Jill had adopted her soothing voice to calm the girl down. "Why did you come to Adams-Larsen?"

Publicly they were a public relations firm.

Privately, they were a whole lot more. As a private witness protection firm, they helped people in danger disappear and relocate in safety. But few people knew that. Because, yeah, their client list was exclusive—not that they didn't take clients who didn't have money, but the criteria for choosing who they helped was specific—and extremely private.

They did have an actual PR department that dealt with high end clients, mostly politicians and wealthy socialites wanting to clean up their image.

But that office was in another facility out in Alexandria.

Tears trembled on the edge of her eyelashes, then spilled down her pale white cheeks. "I heard some rumors about your firm and I did some investigating."

Dwayne glanced at Jill. She gave a slight shake of her head. They worked mainly on referrals. Their billing was done through several shell companies so that even if someone saw the transactions, it would take a talented computer specialist to track down ALIAS's involvement in the disappearance of high-profile individuals.

They'd set it up this way to protect the identity of their clients. And to protect Adams-Larsen from discovery. They'd developed several enemies, even if those enemies had no idea who was behind the disappearance of the people they sought.

Bitsy sniffed. Took a deep breath. With trembling fingers, she wiped away her tears.

The transformation took less than a second, but she went from a mess to composed with a blink. There was more to this girl than first appeared.

Which meant Dwayne needed to do a gut check. This girl had upset Maria. Maria Torres had enough upset in her life she didn't need any more.

What had Bitsy said to Maria?

Bitsy continued, "I'm rather proficient at computer things."

Rather proficient? There was a huge difference between proficiency and the level of computer expertise needed to crack their uber-protected systems. This girl was full of shit. Dwayne waited for Jill to misdirect her.

"Okay," Jill said.

Okay?

Screw that. Bitsy needed to come clean with them. Dwayne crossed his arms, his delts and biceps flexing in annoyance. The girl didn't notice, but for a hot second, Maria's gaze flickered to him and the look in her eyes shocked him. Yearning. Arousal. On anyone else, he'd call it straight-up lust. The hot lick of repressed longing hit him in the solar plexus. Maria was attracted to him?

But then Maria ducked her head again, and Bitsy was clarifying so Dwayne needed to pay attention.

"And I may have overheard a rumor about Adams-Larsen."

Jill tilted her head, almost like she was listening to the girl for evidence of a lie. Dwayne was done. Her language was vague and misleading. He glanced at the tactical watch on his right wrist. "Can we cut to the point?" Sometimes Jillian was too nice.

"My stepfather is friends with Judge Adams." She stared defiantly at them. "And I sometimes overhear things I shouldn't."

Dwayne tightened his lips. Judge Robert "Call Me Bobby" Adams was a pain in their ass. His son—Jillian's partner Marsh—was one of the founders and the guy couldn't seem to keep his mouth shut.

"Have you considered testifying against your stepfather?" Jillian asked carefully.

She scoffed. "I'm the spoiled brat of his current wife. Pretty arm candy without much brain power." Her bird hands clenched the hem of her expensive coat.

Jill pursed her lips, eyed the girl.

"No one will believe me. He'll say I made the whole thing up to try and extort money from him. He scares me," Bitsy finished softly.

Frustration boiled in his gut. He could not get a solid read on this girl.

"So what is it you want us to do for you?"

"Work your magic." Her crystalline emerald-green eyes sparkled. "Make me disappear." As if what they did was a parlor trick and they could wave their hands and get rid of her. Her conspiratorial smile invited them in as if they were all privy to a special secret.

Was Jill seriously falling for this? If it were up to him,

he'd kick this girl to the curb. Tell her she was full of shit, and not to let the door hit her in the ass.

But Jill said, "We could help you step back for a few weeks while you decide what you want to do. We've got a… house we use on occasion for a client who needs to wait until the heat from their public relations issue dies down."

"A few weeks?" Bitsy said doubtfully.

Jill's gray stare was hard as the granite countertop in the ALIAS kitchen. "You would have to cut all ties to your current life while you figure out what you plan to do, and sign a nondisclosure based on the location of the house."

It was almost like Jill was suggesting a test run. This wasn't how they usually handled potential clients. First and foremost, they did a significant amount of background checks and pre-work before they met with a client. The client had already been vetted and cleared before they discussed safe houses and details. Bitsy Vandenbeek was like a freaking walk-in.

ALIAS didn't do walk-ins.

Not to mention this girl was seriously connected. She was likely on the register of Who's Who in society. She might not have paparazzi following her around, like they did with his sister Teuila who was a famous model. But he'd bet his signed Super Bowl football that when her picture got snapped, she was identified by name on Page Six of the *New York Post*.

Most of their clients were unknown beyond their limited news cycles and geographic area. But this girl was high profile on steroids.

"You understand what I'm telling you here, Bitsy?" Jill tapped a French-manicured fingernail against her mouth. "You won't be able to contact your mother, or your friends, or boyfriend."

With every word out of Jill's mouth, Maria had tensed, her body wound tighter. Dwayne wasn't sure why he was here since it was clear Jill had already made up her mind. Almost as if she knew Bitsy was coming.

Bitsy laughed. "Believe me, that isn't a hardship."

Maria jerked.

"I doubt Jason Carlisle Peterson III will miss me," she tossed off flippantly.

This girl was blowing off the hard part of a relocation, even if it was temporary, like it was a fly buzzing around her face, annoying but inconsequential. With every blasé remark, Maria's head bent lower.

They hadn't even agreed to take her on as a client. Yet.

This was temporary.

Dwayne kept his face blank but he planned on having a WTF? conversation with his boss as soon as Bitsy bolted.

His instincts were buzzing. When he'd worked for the FBI, he'd learned to trust his intuition, and his bullshit detector was off the charts.

"It's going to be difficult." Jill strode to her overlarge desk and sat behind it like a queen claiming her throne. "Especially for someone in your position who is so active."

Maria jammed her left hand into her pocket, her knuckles balled into a fist beneath her tailored chestnut wool pants. Her mouth, bare and pale, tightened.

"I can handle it." The frightened waif who'd entered the office had transformed into the confident society girl now that she'd gotten what she wanted.

Maria had practically stopped breathing. Her chest was still beneath the copper-penny-colored turtleneck sweater that covered her spectacular breasts. He wanted to protect Maria from Bitsy's thoughtlessness.

Jill didn't say a word, just studied Bitsy.

Bitsy reached into her ridiculously large leather tote bag with buckles and a shiny gold tag that likely cost more than Dwayne made in a month. She pulled out a wallet with a logo he'd seen in the *Vogue* magazines his sister, La'ei, constantly pored through. As if she sensed Jill's reluctance, Maria's frustration, and Dwayne's skepticism, she waved her wallet. "I can pay you."

"That's not the issue," Jill said.

"I know!" Bitsy whipped around in her seat so quickly, her brown-caramel-blond hair flew out in an arc. She clapped her hands together. "Maria can help me."

Maria's head jerked up, her gorgeous stippled eyes widening and her plump lips rounding in an O.

Hell to the no.

Dwayne surged to his feet and his chest expanded as he got ready to blast this insensitive witch. "What?"

Bitsy shrank back against the settee. But he didn't care.

He hated everything about this situation. Especially Bitsy with her flippant attitude and her blatant disregard for Maria's feelings. As if Maria didn't matter except in relation to how she could be of use to her.

His protective inclinations surged, the need to defend, to shelter her instinctive, yet, unwanted.

"MARIA CAN BE MY MENTOR," Bitsy said gleefully.

Her, in the field? Not locked in the office or her safe apartment.

Maria's first impulse was to head for the door. Her heart thudded with a combination of fear and…excitement?

"Maria isn't field certified," Dwayne ground out. His normal smiling countenance had morphed into a frown, his black eyebrows meeting between his eyes, the laugh lines around his dark eyes crinkling in displeasure.

She'd never seen him unhappy or upset. He was the most even-tempered, easygoing person in the office. Nothing rattled him. He had a carefree smile and a laugh for everyone.

"Dwayne makes a good point," Jill said.

Maria should speak up, turn down Bitsy's request. Her in the field was ludicrous. It was insanity. But even as she opened her mouth to say no, a restless energy filled her.

She wasn't sure what was next. While she appreciated the receptionist job, it was a stopgap until she figured out what to do with her life. Maybe it was time to take some risks.

She was more than the scared woman who had taken far too long to escape her prison.

But she'd done it. She'd rescued herself.

"She knows what it's like. She can help me adjust." Bitsy's words were nearly a whine.

Her circumstance was the opposite of Bitsy Vandenbeek's. She hadn't had a choice about forsaking her life. Her family, her friends had slowly disappeared from her reality as her hope of being rescued had faded. But if she'd had access to a phone, to a computer, she would have contacted them right away. She would have used those tools to escape and return to her life.

The fact that Bitsy could so flippantly speak about leaving everything behind hurt. Even if it was just temporary. Maria wanted to challenge her, to tell Bitsy she had no idea what it was like to lose everything. But the words balled in her throat, her muscles swelling with regret and loss, trapped by her own limitations and inability to speak up.

Deep in her soul Maria knew Bitsy didn't understand but the rage that overwhelmed her at random triggers bubbled, fizzing through her bloodstream, filling her mind with a pure incandescent fury.

Maria kept her head. She couldn't turn that anger on a client. So, she blasted Dwayne—who clearly didn't think she could handle this—with a resting bitch face stare.

Dwayne blinked but didn't back down. Figures the one time he spoke in anger was to believe she couldn't do something.

But he was wrong. She *could* do this.

No one in the room spoke.

Bitsy slumped, sighed. Tears poured from her eyes. "I just want to escape. I'm terrified he's going to kill me too," she whispered. "I don't want to die."

Her muttered statement was the most honest she'd been since she arrived.

"I'll consider your request." Jill patted her on the shoulder.

What? Did Jill mean that Maria would go with Bitsy? Or did she mean Bitsy's request for relocation?

Maria shifted away from the sheer desperation bleeding from Bitsy. As if the girl's insecurity and anxiety could ooze from her and slither into Maria. She couldn't afford to be infected by Bitsy's overblown emotions.

"Please," Bitsy begged.

Jill clasped the girl's hand between her own. "We'll help you figure out what to do next."

Bitsy radiated giddy relief.

"In the meantime, you can't tell anyone about this visit. And you can't breathe a word about going away."

"I won't. I promise."

"Do you have a place you could stay that is away from

your stepfather, at least for the next forty-eight hours? And can you misdirect your friends and family about where you're going?"

"He's supposed to be out of town for a few days. As far as being gone, I can say I'm going to New York for spa days." Bitsy bounced on the blue settee. "I do that regularly so it won't be suspicious."

"What about work?"

"I send my columns for the Post in remotely so it's not a problem."

She treated her upcoming relocation like a grand adventure. This girl was in for a rude awakening.

Jill reached into the filing cabinet drawer in her desk and pulled out an agreement. "Before we go any further, you need to sign a nondisclosure form. This is legally binding, and we will prosecute if you reveal the contents to anyone."

Maria had never signed a nondisclosure agreement and she had been a client of ALIAS before she'd been the receptionist. Jill had offered her a new life, relocation and a new identity if she'd wanted it but Maria had turned her down.

She refused to let José Fernandez take anything else from her.

He'd destroyed her life in the pursuit of power.

So now, Maria, the kidnapped daughter of migrant workers from Mexico lived in Washington, DC and worked for the ultimate in power brokers. She wondered if José Fernandez pondered that irony from his jail cell.

Jill handed Bitsy the nondisclosure agreement.

Bitsy's eyes widened. "Can I have my lawyer look it over?"

"No," Jill said patiently. "That would defeat the purpose

of us protecting you. We take our client's, and our own, privacy very seriously."

"Oh." Bitsy laughed excitedly. "Good point."

She scanned the two-page document, making notations on the contract with sharp, concise strokes.

"You seem very comfortable with the contract." Dwayne's comment was accusation rather than compliment.

"I worked as a receptionist in a law firm for a couple summers." She brushed aside his suspicion. "I used to read contracts during lulls in my day. I picked up some terms."

"Huh. My sister, Sefina, is a lawyer. Her days as an intern were intense and she had to study to pick up terms."

Dwayne seemed to be needling her. Finally she found someone he appeared to like less than Maria.

"Excellent," Jill jumped in. "Then you understand the ramifications of violating the agreement."

Bitsy made another scrawled notation on the contract. When she got to the end, she signed the binding document with a flourish.

As part of her job duties, Maria had obtained her notary license, so she filled out her book, checked Bitsy's ID, and noted her official name, Elizabeth Wilhelmina Stanhope Vandenbeek, on the line. No wonder Bitsy went by the nickname.

Jill gestured to Maria to take notes. "Let's get some information from you and then we'll get started on hiding you temporarily." She sent Dwayne a cautionary look and paced the antique carpet in her shiny patent leather pumps. "Do you have any reason to think that your stepfather suspects you know about his girlfriend?"

Bitsy bit her lip. The shiny gloss had worn off, leaving her not quite as polished and put together as she had been when she'd entered. Maria's inadequacy eased. Beneath her polish and glitz, perhaps Bitsy was more like her than she'd initially thought.

Bitsy said, "I don't think so."

Her response didn't inspire confidence.

"So with your stepfather out of town, we have a day or so to hammer out a plan," Jill said. "If his schedule changes, you need to let me know right away."

"Of course."

"Dwayne, get started on logistics."

"Yes, boss." Dwayne hadn't so much as glanced at Maria, ignoring her. Kind of like he usually did. But this time his avoidance seemed as angry as his gritted teeth.

"Bitsy, we'll be in touch later today."

The girl smiled tremulously. "Thank you."

"Maria, alert the team. We'll assemble in one hour."

Maria nodded. Whatever Jill decided about Maria's participation, Bitsy's relo was going to happen.

"Maria, you stay. Dwayne escort Bitsy to her car."

The door closed behind Dwayne and Bitsy.

Jill assessed Maria. She resisted the urge to fidget. "What do you want to do?"

Jill was leaving it up to her? A fierce longing swelled inside her. She could do this. She could. "I want to do it."

"Bitsy certainly seems comfortable with you." Jill tapped a finger on the blotter of her desk.

Bitsy identified with Maria. Who knew why since their situations were nothing alike. But the brain was a weird place.

"I can do it." With every second Jill was silent the tension built inside Maria. Her earlier hesitation was gone. She could do this. Even more. She wanted to do it.

"I have no reservations about your capability." But it

sounded like she had concerns about something else. Maria waited for Jill to expand on them.

"Okay. You're in."

Maria wanted to fist pump, but she kept her face reserved, knees together, fingers tight on the steno pad.

Yes! She was in.

Chapter Three

The ALIAS team gathered in their conference room, which was the old dining room of the brownstone, outfitted with a large oval mahogany table, a sideboard laden with a silver coffee urn, a hot water urn for tea and hot chocolate, and white ceramic coffee cups with the Adams-Larsen logo and a tray of cookies Maria brought in. Every employee who wasn't out on assignment was in attendance. The other founder, Marsh Adams, was among those absent.

Kita Kim sat to Maria's right with a huge smile on her face. These days it seemed as if she was always smiling.

Dwayne snuck up behind Kita and wrapped an arm around her collarbones and squeezed. Her smile widened. "How's the Fed treating you?" he growled.

Kita rolled her eyes. "Don't make me flip you."

Kita was their resident martial arts expert and she taught self-defense classes to women at a shelter.

Dwayne laughed, his cheeks rising, amusement sparkling in his dark eyes. "You could try, little girl."

Maria watched their interaction. What had she ever done to be denied his brand of teasing?

Dwayne was big—larger than life some days—with a hearty laugh and a quick, bright smile. Her body zinged with awareness whenever he was nearby. Her skin flushed and her nipples tightened. She ached for things she read about in the romance novels she devoured.

But in addition to the sexual feelings, her neck tightened and her throat closed every time Dwayne came within five feet of her.

Between that and his avoidance of her, she had no hope that he'd ever notice her as anything but a freak.

"Get me a cookie," Kita demanded.

Dwayne scooped up several pumpkin-shaped sugar cookies with orange royal icing and green piped frosting for the stem from the platter and handed them out, then he sat opposite Maria. As far away as he could get.

Kita scarfed down the treat. "Jeez, these are good." She sent a chin lift Maria's way. "Thanks."

Maria's heart warmed, expanded. Since she escaped she had so much time on her hands that she'd begun baking. Cookies were her favorite.

Bliss Stone, former ALIAS employee who now headed the West Coast partnership between Adams-Larsen and Stone Consulting, Bliss's husband's company, was on a laptop via Skype. She had reconnected with her former flame on a joint mission to protect Maria and bring José Fernandez to justice.

The laptop was on the sideboard, next to the plate of cookies. Bliss sat at a massive desk with a view of the Monterey Bay behind her, and Jack Stone in a chair off to the side. They were laughing about something while everyone waited for the meeting to start.

"How are you, Maria?" Bliss stared directly into the laptop camera.

She ducked her head. "Fine. Good."

A sliver of concern edged over Jack's face. "You been to the range lately?"

Maria had learned how to shoot a weapon while they'd been in Las Vegas for Bliss and Jack's wedding. She didn't like guns, but she liked knowing she had the skills if she needed to shoot one. "Every two weeks."

Out of her peripheral vision, she saw Dwayne's eyebrows shoot up.

"Excellent." Happiness practically glowed from Bliss.

Before Bliss could ask another question, Viktor Kuznets, their on-site medic, hustled into the conference room. "Sorry I'm late."

Jill gestured to the sideboard. "Get a drink, then we'll get started."

Dwayne and Viktor exchanged some sort of complicated handshake finishing with a fist bump. "Hey man, how's it hanging?"

"Good." Viktor fixed two cups of tea with a brisk tink of the spoon on the ceramic. Then he sat next to Maria and handed her a cup.

She smiled shyly at Viktor, who was sweet, kind, and intense. Of all the people at ALIAS, he made Maria look chatty.

Dwayne glowered at Maria and Viktor from across the expanse.

Jill stood at the head of the table. "We have an unusual situation."

"What about Marsh?" Bliss piped up from the laptop.

Kita and Jill exchanged a look. "He's out on a hush relo."

That explanation had been rolled out enough lately that everyone nodded, but the mood in the room shifted. Something was going on with Marsh Adams. And no one seemed to be talking about it.

Jill concisely laid out Bitsy's visit and the plans to hide her.

They'd covered most of the details of Bitsy's case. Maria still couldn't always wrap her brain around the fact that Adams-Larsen relocated people in danger and set them up with a new life. But if anyone knew that sometimes life was dangerous, it was her.

Kita commented, "This is non-standard practice for us."

"I'm aware." Jill brushed the statement aside.

Kita shrugged. "Okay then. We need selfies of Bitsy so I can pepper her social media feeds with pics of her in New York and no one suspects she's somewhere else." Kita banged furiously on her laptop while the conversation swirled around them.

"Kita can start the Twitter seedings and design some Instagram pictures for New York."

The social media component, misdirecting attention away from where their clients were, helped keep them safe. Even though most of the websites people posted online hadn't been as prevalent when she'd been abducted, she'd become intimately familiar with them over the past year.

"Why do people let everyone know where they are?" They made themselves vulnerable to stalking, to capture, to being hunted.

Dwayne dipped his chin in agreement, but Jillian just smiled. "It's the ephemeral wish for connection…or to show off." She laughed softly. "It certainly makes our job easier."

True.

Kita was a master at misdirection, leading anyone who was searching for their clients in the opposite direction.

Maria was taking notes, but when Jill stopped for a moment, Bliss teased Kita about her new guy. "So, Kita, we need details on this marshal dude."

Kita said slyly, "After you cough up intel about your gorgeous husband."

Jack laughed.

"Why don't you tell them about Jack's lucky desk?" Jill suggested blandly.

Jack's smile disappeared. He raised his eyebrows and shot a look at Bliss, who was blushing furiously.

Bliss deflected quickly, "The house will be ready for you."

They were going to use a house owned by the Stone family. They had houses all over the country.

"Fridge will be stocked and I ordered the cleaning service to come in." Bliss smiled. She looked…happy, content.

Maria had met Bliss after she escaped and Adams-Larsen put her in a safe house. But she'd been terrified and bolted. Bliss and Jack had tracked her down and helped her during the ordeal of José Fernandez's arrest and imprisonment.

Bliss had tried to become a mentor, but Maria was embarrassed to admit that she hadn't let the woman in. Bliss couldn't ever seem to get past the idea that Maria was a victim.

"Perfect." Jill ticked a box on her phone. "Thank you. I know it's last minute."

"Anything else on this end?" Bliss leaned back in her chair, tapping her pen on the blotter of the massive wood desk.

Side conversations were going on around Maria, and she figured they were close to being done with the meeting.

She still couldn't believe that Bitsy wanted her as part of her detail. Jill hadn't communicated her decision to the team yet. But as the idea settled, Maria got more excited. She needed to get out of her comfort zone and start figuring out what she was going to do with her life. She couldn't just bake cookies.

They all waited for Jillian to continue, and Maria figured this was it. As much as she shouldn't care, the ALIAS team's opinion mattered.

"If the house is set, we're good. The client and Kita are heading there in two days on a private jet." Then, Jill dropped her bomb. "Dwayne and Maria will flying commercial slightly ahead of them and make sure the house is ready."

All conversation stopped.

Like a wave, everyone turned toward Maria. Mouths dropped open, the startled surprise on their faces an unwelcome reminder that Dwayne wasn't the only one who might believe she couldn't do this.

The silence stretched on as if no one wanted to be the first to caution her.

Her heart constricted, shrinking in her chest until she thought the weight would crush her.

"Way to go." Kita held her hand up for a high five as a huge smile broke across her face.

Maria blinked.

Viktor patted her hand. "You'll do great."

Jill didn't smile but Maria had worked with her long enough to see her pleasure in the way she held her gaze and nodded. She was thrilled that the rest of the team was supporting Maria.

Dwayne was the only one who wasn't proclaiming how great her entry into the field would be.

"We'll be close if you need help," Bliss said. "Shane can fly us there quickly."

Jill nodded. "There's a low possibility of danger on this mission. It's mostly a cooling-off period for the client. No one is aware of Bitsy's knowledge and they'll be holed up in the house." She tapped a French manicured finger against her lips.

Maria worried at the rosary beads in her pocket. Her mother's. All she had left of her family. She wasn't religious. No just God would have let José Fernandez get away with his crimes. No just God would take everyone away from her and abandon her.

She hadn't seen her mother in nine years. Her parents had been devastated and broken-hearted when she hadn't been found. They'd moved back to Mexico. Her father had been killed and her mother's health and mental acuity had deteriorated to the point that she could no longer travel.

The rosary had arrived in the mail the day José Fernandez had gone to prison.

Maria was all alone. That reality hurt. Of course she had friends, people who were happy she was still around, but she had trouble connecting with them.

"What is wrong with everyone? She is nowhere near ready or capable of going in the field," Dwayne blurted out.

Her heart jerked in her chest at his outburst.

Wonderful. The only one who didn't think she could do this was her partner. She firmed her mouth and straightened her shoulders. He might be an overgrown ex-football player who could crush her between his massive biceps, but she refused to let him count her out.

Maria shoved back her chair and bounced to her feet.

She wasn't going to take his attitude sitting down and at a disadvantage.

"Look. I'm sorry. It's not that you aren't awesome." Dwayne held up his palm as if he could hold her off.

"Too little, too late," Bliss muttered but the whole room heard her.

Dwayne's face twisted. "Shit. I just don't—"

"No one tells me what I can and can't do." Maria's pulse thudded in the base of her throat, not from embarrassment or desire, but from rage.

"Everyone calm down." Jillian had also risen. "Dwayne, I appreciate your concerns, but that's the plan."

Maria and Dwayne turned toward Jill at the same time. Pleasure flushed through her. *Someone* had confidence in her. Wait, she had confidence in herself. She had to.

"This assignment requires two people." Jill continued. "Bitsy has clearly taken a liking to Maria. And she's a bit high strung."

"You think?" Dwayne's voice rose, his tone belligerent. "I don't understand why we're doing this."

"I know her mother. And I know *of* her stepfather." Jill sat at the conference table and scratched additional notes on a piece of paper.

There was a lot unsaid in that statement.

"We're doing it. And Maria is your partner."

"Okay." Dwayne sighed. "Where are we going to stash Bitsy?"

"Lake Tahoe."

"California?" Suddenly Maria's insistence on helping wasn't quite so shiny. She'd spent eight years imprisoned in a basement near Monterey. She hadn't been back since she moved to DC. She had left California behind, along with her insecurities and the constant monitoring by her new friends, who worried about her twenty-four-seven.

Too many memories. All of them bad.

Of course, she'd never been to Tahoe, but it was still way too close to the scene of the worst years of her life.

Dwayne rounded on Maria, as if he'd just been looking for a logical reason to dissuade her from going on this mission. "You want to go back to California?"

Of course she didn't, but she'd be damned if she'd let him know that.

She shoved her chin up, put her fists on her hips, and firmed her resolve. She would do this. "It won't be a problem."

Dwayne ducked his head and rubbed his hand over his smooth scalp. His biceps flexed. She tried, and failed, not to notice. He was hot. Totally hot, and she'd have to be dead not to be drawn to him on a physical level.

She hoped no one else could see her visceral attraction to her coworker.

She wanted to lose her V card, yeah, she'd been watching and reading pop culture, trying desperately to catch up on all that she'd lost, and Mr. Player would be an excellent candidate, if he would notice she was a woman.

But instead he treated her like a girl, a naïve girl who was afraid of her own shadow. Okay, maybe she was afraid, but she kept going no matter how afraid she was.

"Great." Jill interrupted. "Maria, set up plane tickets for the two of you to the Reno/Tahoe airport for tomorrow. Also, book a plane ticket for Bitsy to JFK for her fictitious spa trip." Jill continued to spit out orders. "We'll have her go through security for her trip to New York, then we'll shift her to the private plane and fly straight to the small Truckee Tahoe airport."

"Are you sure this is necessary?" Dwayne stared Maria down.

Jill said, "Based on my knowledge of the situation and Bitsy's family, I have reason to believe she would be in danger if Niles Vandenbeek found out she knows about the murder."

Huh. She hadn't given a single clue when Bitsy had been here. Maria needed to remember that while Jillian Larsen could be warm and accepting, she also had the cool mind and temperament of a master strategist.

Dwayne continued to stare at Maria. She waited, ready to blast him if he started in again on her unsuitability. She tilted up her chin and crossed her arms. His concentration wavered, his gaze dropped to her breasts and heated. Warmth spread through her like a bonfire on a crisp fall night.

"Good," Jill said. "Because you're going undercover as a couple in Tahoe. And I need you both to be able to act like it."

What?

Maria's heart banged against her ribcage. Had Jill reached into her private fantasies and pulled out the shiny dream that filled her nightly slumber? Dwayne was going to say no. She braced for his rejection when he said he wouldn't be able to pull off that kind of charade.

But Dwayne didn't say a word.

"Unless anyone has anything else, we're done. Everyone make this assignment priority number one."

The staff nodded silently and exited the room, sending Dwayne sidelong glances as if waiting for him to lose it. Maria sat frozen in the chair. She couldn't leave until Jill indicated there were no additional notes for the job.

"What the hell, Jill?" Dwayne's meaty hands were

clenched as if he was one step away from punching something.

Maria knew it would be something inanimate—she wasn't afraid of him—he would never hurt a woman. At least not physically.

"What are we doing?" he said. "We don't take clients this quickly. Something is off."

Maria huddled down, wishing she were somewhere else.

"Maybe," Jill said calmly. "It's your job to observe Bitsy while you're holed up in Tahoe."

Dwayne rubbed his bald head again as if reaching for some sort of comfort. "Okay, fine."

"Can I count on you to be professional?" Jillian stared at Dwayne hard, and he flushed.

It was the first time Maria had ever seen him at a loss for words.

"Of course," he said stiffly. "It won't be a problem."

"Maria—"

"But you can't let Maria go on this op," Dwayne interrupted.

Bristling, Maria turned to Jill. "I can do this."

"I know." Jill's gray gaze was troubled.

"Are you both insane?" Dwayne blurted out before either woman could speak.

Maria's chest tightened, frustration wrapping around her lungs cutting off her air supply like the black bag her abductors had placed over her head. She clenched the rosary beads so tightly, the edges of the fire agate cut into her palm.

"You think I can't handle it?" She wanted to do this job and help Bitsy, but some days she barely felt like she could help herself. However, she hated the fact that he thought she couldn't do it.

Dwayne winced. "It's not that I don't think you can. You shouldn't *have to* handle this situation." He fumbled through the denial, trying unsuccessfully to dig himself out of the hole.

She stared him down, her gaze locked with his dark, soulful eyes. Finally, she wasn't blushing or dithering in his presence. She was standing up for herself.

Dwayne blinked, looking at a loss for words. She willed him to at least acknowledge her strength.

A strange energy vibrated between them, so intense Maria was hyper focused on him.

"No one is saying you can't handle it," Jill spoke, breaking the weird tension. "Your job is to keep Bitsy calm and stop her from freaking out."

Maria jolted. She'd forgotten Jill, so caught up in Dwayne and the flickers of heat that licked through her body.

Her emotions were all over the place. She wanted to cower in a closet and she wanted to come out swinging. Both odd feelings initiated by the man staring her down.

Dwayne stood to his full, formidable height. He crossed his arms, his biceps flexing and the muscle in his jaw popping. Except this time, she wasn't turned on by his physical strength.

Okay, maybe she was a little turned on.

Her girl parts tingled. He was a beast. In theory she should be afraid of him. He was big—he could overpower her easily—but beneath that muscled exterior and menacing frown, was a caretaker.

She'd overheard him on the phone with his mother one day. He'd been as sweet as freshly set flan. She knew he had a softness inside him. He just didn't show it to her.

Then Dwayne bared his teeth in a rough smile she'd

never seen before. Scary rather than sweet. He said to Jill, "I won't let you down."

"It's not me you need to worry about," Jill said. "It's Maria."

"I won't let anything happen to you." His customary grin was back in place but she could see the underlying irritation. He was dreading this assignment.

She should be too, but instead a sense of optimism infused her. She could do this. It would be another step in building her confidence. And maybe she'd become more comfortable around Dwayne. She couldn't resist adding, "I won't let anything happen to you either."

His smile disappeared.

Chapter Four

Dwayne was running late.

That never happened. He was the protector, the planner, the one who mapped out contingencies and prepared for them. His backup plans had backups. But even he could not have foreseen the past half hour.

Bitsy had called in a panic. Their timetable accelerated after Jill determined that Bitsy was in imminent danger. But before they could leave, Jill had demanded an off-the-books meeting, so here he was.

He scurried into Jill's office, shooting a surprised glance at Maria's empty desk.

"Where's Maria?"

"She's off getting a small makeover and an appropriate wardrobe. You'll pick her up at her apartment."

Dwayne swallowed.

She was already wonderfully, off-the-charts attractive. What else could they do?

"Have a seat." Jill gestured to the small settee, but Dwayne deliberately sat in the chair Maria had occupied during their earlier meeting.

"What's up?"

"I need you to run a counter-mission." But she didn't sound happy about it.

Dwayne frowned. Waited.

"We need to convince Bitsy to come back to DC before next Monday."

"What's next Monday?"

"A House committee meeting with pharmaceutical CEOs including her stepfather to discuss the recent rampant increases in prescription drug prices."

"Bitsy wouldn't be called to testify at a committee hearing. She's not officially employed by Van Pharma."

"No. But after Vandenbeek testifies, he's going to be arrested."

"Still not computing."

"A Grand Jury will be convened. The attorneys want to depose Bitsy *before* he's arrested."

"I thought you said she was in danger." He was trying to understand but everything about this particular case was confusing.

"She is." Jill rubbed her palms along her pencil skirt.

Nervous? His boss didn't get nervous. "Jill?"

"We need her to share her information with the FBI."

"I thought the plan was to keep her safe and you didn't care if she spoke with authorities."

"No. I didn't want *her* to know that she needs to tell the FBI what she knows."

"Okay. Then why not bring this up in the employee meeting?" He was missing something important.

"I'd prefer to keep this low pressure. I don't want to push Maria."

"You believe she can handle this?"

"It's low risk, as long as Bitsy's stepfather doesn't find out where she is." Jill shifted her gaze to the bookshelves along the wall of the office. "And we've taken the necessary precautions."

That wasn't an answer.

Jill propped against her desk and crossed her long legs at the ankles. "Maria Torres has more courage than everyone at ALIAS combined."

Dwayne wasn't about to argue with his boss. But damn, he wanted to.

"I wouldn't send her if I didn't think she could handle it. In the year since she escaped, she put her captor in jail, moved across the country, got her GED, and overcame nearly insurmountable odds to function and live in a strange city. If she wants to do this, I am not going to hold her back," Jill said fiercely.

Dwayne lifted his palms up in a classic gesture of surrender.

"But I am counting on you to look out for her."

Dwayne had enough responsibilities in his personal life. His mother and six sisters depended on him to be the head of the household, to keep everyone on track and safe. He didn't need another responsibility. He opened his mouth to object.

"I get that you have family obligations." Jill surprised him. He didn't talk about that much but the timing on his resume was pretty obvious and everyone knew he'd quit Notre Dame football and come home after 9/11. "And that you're reluctant to take on more, but I need you."

And with that one request, she'd hooked him.

"I also need you to get information about Niles Vandenbeek's business practices."

Dwayne raised his eyebrows. "While we're in Tahoe?"

"Bitsy is smart. But her stepfather tends to diminish her

accomplishments. He's a traditional misogynist who refuses to acknowledge female intelligence. Women are supposed to be arm candy."

Her eyes narrowed, and if looks could kill, Niles Vandenbeek would be in mortal danger right now.

Anger puffed out his chest, burning beneath his breastbone. His father had taught him the value of women and his mother had shown him true strength when she kept his family from crumbling after his father's death.

"The committee also wants to investigate immoral practices used by lobbyists to increase their clients' profits. That's why Vandenbeek had his mistress murdered. Someone tipped him off to the upcoming investigation. We need to mine Bitsy's brain and her memories to see if she can help make a case for prosecution."

That niggle that something else was going on beneath the surface returned.

"You got it."

Jill placed her palm over his clenched fist. "I know I can count on you."

"Of course."

But his stomach had cramped at the thought of deceiving Maria. So here he was, with a counter-mission in place and the need to hide things from his partner while still protecting her without making it look like he was protecting her. That short, but full of impact, meeting had put him way behind schedule.

Dwayne swung by Maria's impersonal apartment complex and texted her.

She must have been waiting by the door because as soon as he drove up, she strode out pulling a fancy roller suitcase behind her.

He nearly swallowed his tongue.

Damn, she looked amazing. She had on a wool coat that hit at the knees revealing her bare legs and sleek ankles. Her feet were clad in sexy red pumps.

He exited the driver's side and rounded the car. "I've got this."

She hesitated before letting go of the suitcase handle.

"We've got to make one stop before we leave." Dwayne tossed the dark purple suitcase in the trunk next to his small utilitarian case.

Maria blinked. "Where?"

"I have to stop by my mother's house before we head to the airport."

His mother, who was going to get the wrong impression from meeting Maria. But it couldn't be helped.

Dwayne drove on the edge of the speed limit. The silence in the car was comfortable, easy, despite the fact that tension rode his shoulders hard.

Within twenty minutes they were at his childhood home. "You want to wait in the car?"

"Whatever is easiest."

But that wasn't what she wanted. He could practically see the longing on her face. "Come on in, this won't take long."

They strode up the plain cement walkway. Fall flowers sat in an urn on the front porch and a grapevine wreath with silk leaves in fall colors decorated the front door.

Dwayne walked right in.

Maria paused in the doorway.

Shoes littered the entryway and tumbled out of a big plastic tub next to the front door. Three of his sisters still lived at home. "I'm here. I don't have much time—last-minute change of plans," he yelled as he made a beeline for the kitchen.

The old refrigerator was plastered with pictures of him and his sisters growing up. A toaster oven, coffeemaker, and blender cluttered the counters. Handmade ceramic blobs from fifth-grade art class huddled with jars of Mama's favorite spices. The scuffed linoleum floors and stained grout between the countertop tiles spoke of the hub of his family home.

"Tupua!" His mother bustled toward him and enveloped him in a tight hug. The smell of vanilla and flour and Dove soap surrounded him. The scent of love and acceptance. "And who is this?"

Discomfort trickled through him at the gleam in his mother's eye. "Mama. This is Maria. From work."

"Maria." Dwayne had spoken about Maria, about her ordeal, to his family. His mother barreled toward a wide-eyed Maria and circled her arms around her. "You poor darling."

Mama squeezed Maria tight but she just stood there, stock-still, as if unsure how to respond to his mother's affection. And fuck, he never thought about it before, but she'd been in solitary confinement for eight years. He had no idea where her family was. Or who worried about her now.

She always held herself slightly apart. It occurred to him that he rarely saw her touch anyone.

"My Tupua will take care of you. Don't you worry." Mama patted her on the back.

Slowly Maria's arms crept around his mama's waist. But she didn't hold on. As if she were too afraid to show any longing for touch, any wish for compassion.

"Tupua?" Maria's muffled voice came from the rolls of his mother's neck.

"My Samoan name," he answered. "Dwayne is my

American name." For teachers and coaches who thought his real name was too difficult to pronounce. Insert eye roll. But it was fine. He'd chosen his American name after his idol. Dwayne "The Rock" Johnson.

"Ah."

"We have to go."

She nodded and let go of Maria. "I know you do, sweet boy."

Dwayne heard Maria's muffled snort. She smoothed her hands over her hair, patting the dark curls back into order.

"Thank you for indulging me."

Dwayne flushed. "Of course. I'll let you know when I'm back in town. But it might be a while."

"Will you be home for church?"

His family tried to attend church together on Sundays and then they gathered for dinner. He rarely missed it unless he was out of town. He wanted to confirm he would be here.

Jill's counter-mission directive echoed in his head, twisted in his gut. Going into an op with a secret from his partner was not his normal modus and he hated it.

"Not unless something changes."

His mother's face fell. "We will miss you."

"Me too, mama."

"Nice to meet you, sweetheart." Mama hugged Maria one more time.

"Nice to meet you too, Mrs. Lameko."

"None of that." His mother flicked her hand. "Call me Mama."

Maria's smile barely graced her mouth.

"Bye, Mama. Tell the brood I'll be back." Dwayne wrapped his arms around his mother's ample waist again, and her familiar embrace washed over him. That touchstone—the superstition that everything would be fine, as long as they maintained their connection and said goodbye in person—eased his soul.

"Thank you for honoring your commitment," she whispered against his chest. "*Ia e saogalemu.*" Be safe.

"Always." Dwayne bussed the side of his mother's head, squeezed for a fraught moment, then let her go. They needed to motor.

Mama clasped her hands together and smiled at Maria. "Take care of this one." Her dark eyes sparkled with hope. His mother was destined to be disappointed.

"Of course." Dwayne escorted Maria to the car. While he opened her car door, he tossed the words over the hood of the car. "*Alofa atu, Mama.*"

She stepped back, her eyes suspiciously bright.

Once Maria was buckled in, he shot away from the curb. "Thanks. Sorry about the delay."

Maria didn't even look at him. But her unspoken question hovered in the tense air between them.

"My, ah, father died in a plane crash. On 9/11."

"Oh." She sucked in a breath.

"It's a family ritual. I always say goodbye in person before I leave on a trip."

"What did you say to her? Sow-ga-lay-mu?"

"It means Be Safe in Samoan."

"And the other…a-low-fa?"

"I said I love you."

"That's…."

He didn't want to hear whatever was going to come out of her mouth.

"Sweet," she sighed.

Sweet? He wasn't sweet. He was a big badass mother… lover. Okay maybe it was sweet. But still.

"We'll have to go through security separately," he said brusquely.

"Wait. Why?"

Dwayne's stomach curdled. "I'm taking my firearm with me."

"Do you think you'll need it?" Her voice held curiosity, not fear. And he wanted to keep it that way.

"Precautionary." Unless Bitsy was discovered in Tahoe. Then all bets were off. The fact that they'd moved up their timetable with less prep than ever before didn't necessarily bode well for an incident-free assignment.

"Your mother seems nice."

He laughed, from his belly. His Mama was crazy, controlling, and sometime a pain in his ass and *nice* typically wasn't what came to mind.

"Why is that funny?"

"She's a hard ass."

Maria bristled.

"She had to be. She kept all seven of us in line after my papa died."

Dwayne had helped. At eighteen, he'd been the oldest. He'd given up his football dreams, playing at Notre Dame and hoping for pro career, to come home to study at the local community college. He'd lived at home and helped keep his sisters in line. School had been an afterthought, but then he'd found his calling when he changed his major to criminal justice.

September eleventh had altered the trajectory of his life. But he wouldn't change where he was now. He loved working for ALIAS. The FBI had been too restrictive, justice had been tangled up in red tape and bureaucracy. The work with their clients at ALIAS was hands-on. And the satisfaction was immediate and gratifying as opposed to the slow process of putting white collar criminals away.

"Seven?" Maria's voice rose.

"Me and…six sisters."

"Six. Wow. I had no idea," she said faintly.

"It keeps life interesting." He loved his sisters. But they were a lot to take in some days. He wondered if she had any siblings. "I realized I don't know much about you."

She laughed harshly. "Yeah, being a freak who was kidnapped tends to wipe everything else out of people's minds."

He wanted to soothe her. Odd, he rarely had that reaction around anyone but family. Except, he didn't have brotherly feelings toward her. Based on her body language, sympathy was the last thing she wanted, even if she needed it.

"Family?"

"Not anymore." Her earlier vivaciousness had disappeared, her burled mahogany eyes clouded.

"What happened?"

"My parents fell apart after I disappeared. Eventually they moved back to Mexico. My father was killed."

"Killed?"

"Wrong place, wrong time."

"What about your mother?"

She fingered something in her pocket. "She…isn't doing well."

But she had seen her, right? Family was everything and his heart hurt for her. "I'm sorry."

She glanced out the car window. "Yeah, well, what are you going to do?"

Chapter Five

What had she been thinking?

Maria minced along beside Dwayne on four-inch heels, dressed in an expensive cashmere, wraparound dress that bared more of her chest than she was used to. Jill had sent her to a salon where they'd added some caramel highlights to her dark hair and scrubbed and pinched and exfoliated her face and upper chest until she glistened. She'd been slathered with fruity-smelling lotions. They'd put some hard polish stuff on her nails, shellac in a "notice me" red she would have never chosen.

Being noticed made her skin crawl.

She tended to blend. Even with her new wardrobe and brighter colors, she didn't stand out. Didn't want to. Being singled out from her friends had gotten her eight years in confinement. While they'd been forced to do unspeakable things, Maria had just been sequestered away from people. José Fernandez had known her parents. He'd been appalled when he discovered she'd been kidnapped too. To appease his guilt, Fernandez had not sold her into slavery, which caused her buckets of remorse. Her friends had not been so lucky. And every day her shame ate at her conscience. So no, she didn't like being singled out.

Between her brightly patterned dress and Dwayne by her side, she was receiving attention.

Idiot that she was, she was the one to insist that she could do this. That she could help watch Bitsy in Tahoe. That she was strong enough, capable enough.

What the hell had she been thinking?

So here she was trying and failing miserably to follow her crush, coworker—*coworker*, she reminded herself again—and pretend that they were a couple.

Except for the brief stop at his mother's house, Dwayne had barely acknowledged her existence. He'd spent the rest of the drive to the airport on his cell talking to his sister, Lulu, helping her through her accounting homework. Sweet. Even if he didn't like the designation.

He was sweet.

Yeah, she got it. He didn't want her here. Didn't think she could do the job, no matter what their boss said.

The gorgeous shoes pinched her toes and her legs were getting a better workout than when she logged her daily miles on the treadmill. Dwayne Lameko was a lot taller than her. His strides ate up the distance to their gate like Ms. Pacman eating those dots on the ancient video game machine at her local pizza parlor when she'd been a carefree kid.

"Hey," she said breathlessly. But he didn't turn, didn't even acknowledge her.

Screw it. He wanted to act like a jerk, fine, but her feet hurt and she wasn't about to run to keep up with someone who didn't want her there in the first place.

Dwayne continued to stride along. Maria shook her head, settled the large Louis Vuitton bag in the crook of her elbow, and decided to take her time. Jill had shown her how to walk in the heels so that she swayed rather than tiptoed, and with some practice she'd get the hang of it. So she ignored her reluctant partner and focused on projecting the character of a wealthy woman about to go on a trip.

Dwayne finally realized she wasn't next to him.

He stopped, turned around, and searched. The airport was crowded. She couldn't be sure but she thought she saw panic on his face. As if he'd lost her. Like a parent realizing they'd misplaced their kid in a crowded mall.

When Dwayne's gaze connected with hers, his shoulders relaxed. And he waited.

Maria continued her slow saunter down the terminal hallway. She wanted to squirm at his undivided attention, but she kept her expression serene and hoped he couldn't see how uncomfortable he made her.

"Hey." When she got next to him, she grabbed his forearm before he could take off again. Electricity sizzled through her body. Crazy longing made her chest ache. What if they were a real couple on their way to a romantic getaway in Tahoe? He'd be holding her hand, or maybe he'd curl his arm around her shoulders and snuggle her close to his side, keeping his body between her and the rest of the world.

Dwayne pulled her from the deluge of oncoming passengers. Kind of like her trip into wishful thinking land, he blocked her from the hordes rushing to their planes.

His brows arced together in a frown. "You okay?"

Maria flushed. She'd built a lovely fantasy around a teensy tiny *what if?*

He was so close, and with these killer heels on, she was taller than normal. So tall, she could see the flecks of gold and green in his dark brown eyes. He must have been chewing gum, because the spearmint blew into her mouth when he sighed.

"Of course I'm okay."

Dwayne hadn't looked away from her. His intense regard focused on her, searching for weakness.

She sighed in exasperation. "I'm tougher than I look."

RIGHT NOW, Maria looked like his midnight dreams come to life. He didn't know why the hell Jill thought Maria needed to be dressed in character, but Jill had decided that Maria needed to play the part of a wealthy socialite.

From the tips of her bright red stilettos to the crown of her soft wavy curls now streaked with lighter brown, she looked every inch a woman with money.

She wore a wraparound dress that tied in a bow at her waist, exposing her cleavage, which he hadn't seen before. He definitely would have remembered those gorgeous breasts and the intriguing valley between them. And great, he was perving on his coworker.

The bold colors complemented her skin tone, and her makeup showed off plump lips and gorgeous deep-set eyes that were glaring daggers at him.

"We're supposed to be a couple on vacation," she hissed. "And you're embarrassing me."

Shame flooded him, curling through his limbs and filling up his heart. His attraction wasn't her problem. He needed to get over it. Sure, it had been a while since he'd been undercover, but she was the one acting like a professional while he threw the equivalent of a temper tantrum.

He didn't want her here. Not because he didn't think she couldn't handle it but because she'd had to handle enough things in her life. He had the desire to wrap her up in his protective arms and shelter her from the big bad world.

"You're right." Dwayne cupped her cheek in his palm, marveling at her lush beauty. Of course, he'd been attracted to her without all the fancy trimmings, but now everyone else saw her beauty too, and her lush curves were harder to ignore. "I'm sorry."

Her breath caught, and her eyes held a mixture of defiance and hope. The hollow at the base of her throat pulsed. "I won't break."

Dwayne laughed softly. "You're the strongest woman I know."

She blinked. Blinked again. "So hold my damn hand, *pendejo*."

He laughed louder. "Did you just call me an asshole?"

"If the slur fits." She shrugged, her dress gapping enticingly. Dwayne wanted to groan.

He had the urge to pull the sides of the dress together to hide her from leering eyes. But when he got her alone, he wanted to untie that bow and unwrap her like his very own birthday present.

He wanted to worship her curves with his tongue and play with those breasts until she begged for mercy. Shit. Things like workplace harassment and ethical behavior swirled in his brain. But they couldn't override his reaction to her.

He closed his eyes, tilted his head back. Fought to wrestle his out-of-control hormones back into the forbidden box. "You are going to be the death of me," he muttered.

She held out her hand and wagged it.

He brushed his thumb over her cheekbone, watched that flutter in her throat, then slid his palm down her arm and curled his fingers around hers.

The contact sizzled up his arm and zapped his heart. He liked the feel of her hand in his. Way too much. "Better?" he choked out through a tight throat.

She nodded. "But slow down. These heels are killing me."

"You and me both," he murmured.

"What?"

"Nothing." Dwayne lifted her fingers to his mouth, brushed a soft kiss across her knuckles, mostly to distract her. "*La'u manamea.*"

"What does that mean?"

"Sweetheart."

She arched a brow at him, her warm honey-and-coffee eyes sparkling with mirth. "That's a much nicer pet name than *pendejo*."

"Hey, I'm a nice guy."

Her fingers tightened on his and she sobered. "I know."

A crowd of people deplaning rushed through the suddenly constricted hallway.

He saw the moment it happened.

A man rushing by jostled her, and her already tentative balance thrown off, she stumbled into Dwayne. And the damage was done.

Panic rushed over her face. Her eyes went glassy with fear. Her breath gasped.

Dwayne didn't even hesitate. "I've got you."

Another rattling gasp shook her chest. He half lifted her off her feet and ushered her toward the floor-to-ceiling window next to the gateway. Dwayne spun her around so she faced the window and could see outside, then he caged her protectively.

He bent to talk quietly in her ear. "You're okay. Breathe, *la'u manamea.*"

The endearment slipped out. He wanted to wrap her up in his arms and shield her from the fear that shuddered through her body in great heaving gasps.

"Breathe in, two, three, four." He kept a proper distance between their bodies. "Hold it and then breathe out through your nose."

"So-so-sorry." Her chest rose and fell with each labored gasp.

He blocked out the rest of the terminal, the people, the different languages, the muffled blare of the public address system, the smells from the pretzel cart next to the gate. He met her gaze in the reflection of the glass. "You got this."

She nodded, determination replacing the fear that had all but crippled her.

Within minutes, her breath slowed and her body lost its frozen stiffness.

Maria turned around and opened her mouth to apologize, he'd guess. Screw that. She had nothing to apologize for.

"You're going to be okay." He headed off the apology.

She breathed deep and he tried not to notice the way her breasts lifted and held as if she were waiting for something.

She leaned into his chest, her breasts brushing his pecs, and now he was the one holding his breath. Holy shit, she felt fabulous. Soft, and feminine, and lush against his chest. He wanted to press her up against the glass and do things to her.

Her fingers curled around his biceps, clutching tight because she couldn't wrap all the way around.

He just wanted to distract her but instead she was distracting him.

"Did I screw it up completely?"

"No. But the key to fooling people is to actually become the persona you're using. You're no longer Maria. You've got to act like your undercover character. That woman likes it when people notice her."

"I thought the point of being undercover was to blend?"

"I'm never going to blend, I'm too big. We need to stand out instead."

She jerked a little. "Yeah. See you usually try to blend in. But that's what Maria does. We don't."

She swallowed, her eyes wide as she digested what he was explaining.

He bent closer. Surreptitiously he cased the rest of the terminal. No one was paying any attention to them, but they needed to play the part, just in case.

"What are you doing?" she whispered against his mouth, the puff of air a bigger turn-on than full frontal nudity. Her plump lips so close he wanted to eat her up.

"Going deep into my cover."

She blinked, her surprise in the rounded O of her mouth.

"How?" she said breathlessly.

"By cementing our coupledom." He lifted her fingers to his mouth again. He couldn't kiss her. He wanted it too much.

Her liquid gaze burned with unnamed emotion. "Won't this call too much attention to us?"

He bared his teeth in a predatory smile. "If anyone is watching, they'll remember what we were doing, not what we look like."

SHE WAS GOING TO COMBUST.

At the mere brush of his lips on her fingers, the tingle started low in her belly. Like when she read the racy books on her ereader. She didn't know what to do with the sensations rushing through her like a flash flood.

The flush started at her toes and spread upward. Her face felt hot, uncomfortable. And she was ten million times more dizzy than drinking champagne after that simple touch.

She was an idiot.

He was just acting. She needed to keep reminding herself that it was all make believe.

"Dwayne." Her breathy sigh hit his chest.

His smile was tender, sweet. "I'm not going to let anything happen to you."

But who would protect her from him? She must seem like the most naïve, inexperienced girl on the planet. Unable to handle even a simple caress.

Maria ducked her head. "I can do this." The idea of becoming someone else and disappearing into a character was incredibly appealing. If she could power through his disapproval, she could learn to help people like herself. People in danger. Being able to rescue clients would be amazing.

"I know," he said fiercely. "I shouldn't have objected."

She jerked her head up so fast that she almost clipped him on the chin.

"You're the strongest woman I know."

She clutched his massive biceps. Strong? Her?

"No, I take that back."

See, she knew he couldn't possibly mean that. Her shoulders relaxed.

"You're the strongest *person* I know." He was laser focused on her. The crowds, the noises from the airport faded, and they were enclosed in a capsule of intimacy that caused the rest of the world to disappear.

"I think you're loco."

His skin was warm, pliant under her fingers. So supple and smooth, the urge to run her fingers up and down his arms was nearly an ache. The desire to have the freedom to touch him, the way she'd read about, the way she'd dreamed of for so long, burned.

But before she could follow her impulses, he turned away and led her to their gate. Disappointment wormed its way in through the relief. Make believe. She had to keep remembering it was all make believe.

Would she ever know what it was like to have a man kiss her passionately?

No not any man. She admitted, she didn't want just any man. She wanted Dwayne.

Chapter Six

Maria snuggled into the first-class seat beside him. Her wonder at the luxuriously wide seats and the service as the flight attendant brought the passengers drinks in real glasses was cute. She couldn't fake boredom, and he didn't want to be the one to crush that amazement at something most people would take for granted. Her obvious delight was out of character for the roles they were supposed to be playing, but he didn't care.

There were no direct flights to Reno, so they'd have to fly through Denver. While they traveled in luxury, Bitsy and Kita were flying to New York first to check Bitsy into a hotel and spa. Then Bitsy would quietly disappear. Kita and Bitsy were taking Jack Stone's private plane right to the small regional Tahoe airport. No cameras, light security, and serious privacy.

At that point, Maria would keep Bitsy company while Dwayne stood guard.

He was dreading this assignment for several reasons.

As he spent more time in Maria's presence, his

admiration for her grew. And the more she began to loosen up around him.

She hadn't seemed scared of him since they got to the airport. Which made him less uptight around her.

Dwayne couldn't afford to become distracted by his lovely, admirable coworker. He shifted in the seat, stretching his legs, thankful for the space in the first-class cabin as they waited for takeoff. Since his father's death, he still got a jolt of fear every time he flew.

His heart began to thump. The deep beat reverberated through his chest like a death knell.

His thoughts spiraled into places better left unexplored. He knew it was a bad precedent but every time he was on airplane he wondered about his father's final moments. Wondered if he'd been scared or pissed or regretful. The ways that Dwayne's life changed that day pummeled him all over again. He missed his dad.

For that matter, he missed himself.

Missed that carefree kid who lived for football. Even though he'd never go back to being that kid, the sudden loss of his dreams had taken something he was still trying to gain back.

He'd become head of the household and keeper of seven souls in an instant. Responsibility was what he knew. He didn't resent it but sometimes he wished for more.

The flight attendant paused at their row. "Anything to drink?"

Goddamn he wanted a beer. "Just a sparkling water."

"Of course, and for you?" She leaned closer to Dwayne as she smiled at Maria.

Maria blinked. "Water is fine."

The flight attendant nodded politely.

"You could order a drink."

Just because he didn't want to be impaired didn't mean she couldn't indulge. His stomach churned again as the engines revved.

"I don't know how to drink."

"It's relatively easy."

She flushed and turned away, staring intently out the window.

He realized he'd embarrassed her. "As in you haven't ever?"

"I had half a glass of champagne at Bliss and Jack's wedding," she said softly. "It made me dizzy."

Dwayne hadn't been able to attend the Las Vegas wedding. He'd been on a relo in Texas.

"Did you like it?"

She didn't answer, just kept looking out the window. Dwayne signaled the flight attendant. "Bring us two champagnes." Fuck it. There was enough time between take off in DC and landing in Reno to burn off whatever alcohol he sipped.

Maria shook her head.

The sass that colored their earlier interactions was gone. Dwayne hated that slightly defeated look on her face. He couldn't bear for her to be so down.

He reached across the large console and grabbed her hand. She tried to tug discreetly to escape his hold, but Dwayne wouldn't let her.

Her gaze shot sparks at him, and if looks could incinerate, he'd be toast.

But something happened when her palm met his. A subtle peace flowed through him, as if she'd filled him with calm, with serenity.

His heart rate slowed, settled. The constriction and the

stress eased. Holding her hand became less about her, and more about him.

The plane started pushing away from the gate and he jerked.

"What's wrong?" Maria looked around, seeking the threat.

Now it was his turn to be embarrassed. "Nothing." It was stupid. He knew it.

"It's not nothing."

"Let it go," he ground out.

She tried to tug her hand from his. She balled her fingers into a fist, denying him her touch, and her trust. So he took what he could get and lifted her whole fist to his lips. "I'm an ass."

"No argument there."

Dwayne huffed out a laugh. "Don't candy-coat it, tell me how you really feel."

But she didn't smile. "Can I have my hand back now?"

"Nope."

Their back and forth continued until Dwayne was surprised to realize they were in the air.

"Why are you so tense?" she pushed again. The sick feeling he'd been trying to forget returned.

Fortunately the flight attendant chose now to deliver their drinks. Her face flickered with disappointment as her gaze dropped to their clasped hands.

Dwayne released her fingers and handed Maria her glass and picked up his own. "To first times."

Her face flushed bright red. She took a big gulp, then started coughing. Her breath wheezed in and out.

Shit. That didn't come out right. But a full body flush started in his stomach, spreading out to his extremities as he contemplated why *she* would be blushing so hard.

A virgin. It was logical, and yet he hadn't thought about her sexual experience in detail. He tried not to think Maria and sex in the same sentence.

But his body responded as he considered the possibility that she was untried. He wanted to introduce her to sensual delights.

An ardent fire burned within her and he would love to be the man who stoked those flames into an inferno. The man who showed her passion. The man who led her into the erotic world of sexual desire.

He wanted to be the man who opened her world to a banquet of sensual delights.

Maria licked the champagne from lips stained with burgundy gloss and closed her eyes.

"You like it?" His voice was far huskier than normal.

She nodded without looking at him.

"It's crisp. Sweet, but not too sweet." She took another dainty sip. "I like the way it fizzes on my tongue."

God, he burned with the need to taste her essence accentuated with champagne. Dwayne leaned closer, her earthy perfume surrounded him and her sweet breath puffed against his mouth.

He'd been thinking about kissing her for months.

He was such a horn dog. She didn't need him sniffing around her. But when he pulled away, her eyes drifted open. She blinked. Jerked away from him, but not before he'd seen the disappointment on her face.

Did she want him to kiss her?

This assignment was a train wreck. He'd almost kissed his coworker twice in the past hour. That was not professional. Also not the way to keep her safe.

He needed to keep his mind on the job and off Maria's tempting curves.

Dwayne shut down his longing. He had a job to do. And he couldn't afford the distraction that was Maria Torres.

She pulled out the inflight magazine from the pocket in the seatback and flipped determinedly through the pages.

Dwayne turned on his laptop and opened the financials on Van Pharmaceuticals. He read through several years of reports distributed to their shareholders. He examined their expenses, searching for red flags. The cost of their drugs had gone up due to the increase in the cost of materials. When he dug further into the details, the explanation notated in the report referenced the increase in two components produced by VDBC based out of Switzerland. Dwayne did a search but VDBC was privately held and the information online was sketchy. The scarce press releases stated the company had been in existence for over one hundred years and held in the same family for the concurrent amount of time. But in general terms, the major reason for the increase in the cost of the asthma drugs was the two thousand percent increase in the costs associated with VDBC.

So why wouldn't Van Pharmaceuticals just use a different supplier?

That was a question for Bitsy.

While he was protecting Bitsy, he needed to delve into what she knew about her stepfather's company without jeopardizing her safety. Not to mention his counter-mission to gather intel and convince Bitsy to share her information with the FBI. An unsettled discomfort fizzled through him. He didn't like keeping things from his partner. And for better or worse, he and Maria were partners right now.

Next to him Maria had fallen asleep. She shifted in the seat, drawing his gaze even as his brain puzzled at the financials. In rest, she seemed younger, and so innocent, in no way ready for this job. His heart constricted.

His other job was to protect Maria. Even though she believed she could handle this assignment, he planned on being there in case she had any problems. What concerned him was that his feelings for her were not easy to identify.

He'd defend his family to the death by looking out for his mother, for his sisters. However, he didn't want to add to the list of people who depended on him. He cared about work, but typically he could separate work clients from his family.

Maybe it was because at work he was part of a team. He was one cog and the machinery of ALIAS only worked if everyone performed their function.

That sense of obligation, the determination to protect and insulate his family, didn't carry over to his clients at ALIAS. He was kick ass at his job. He liked the instant gratification of being able to help people escape bad circumstances. But he never felt the same weight of responsibility when he was protecting clients. His family took his time and energy. His mother and six sisters depended on him to be the glue that held them together and kept them from self-destructing.

He didn't have room in his life for more personal responsibility. Jillian had been right. He didn't want to add anyone else to the list of people who depended on him.

But when he looked at Maria, the temptation to do just that burned.

Chapter Seven

Maria tried not to gawk at the specially modified Range Rover waiting for them at the airport.

The overly large SUV was designed for a driver and potential bodyguard up front with screened windows to shield the high-profile passengers in the back. The fancy car, leather seats, separate heating/cooling controls, and massage seats, screamed luxury. It was so far removed from the rusted old pickup truck her parents had driven as to be in a separate galaxy. When she'd been a teen she couldn't even imagine such a lavish vehicle.

Some days she couldn't make the mental leap from her life before her kidnapping…and now.

Her reflection was crisp, clear in the shiny black finish. The expensive smell of brand new car invaded her senses. She'd never ridden in anything so extravagant. She surreptitiously stroked the soft leather, skimming her fingertips along the luxuriousness, her skin tingling at the sumptuousness.

Dwayne threw their bags in the back and hustled to the driver's seat. Once he was situated, they were on their way.

Since they'd landed, the sky had darkened to an ominous slate gray. Clouds hovered close to the ground casting a gloomy pall over the asphalt road. He peered through the windshield at the rapidly changing weather.

"That doesn't look good."

The drive to the cabin took about forty-five minutes. The mountain was beautiful, evergreens and pines dotted the winding road once they left the main highway, revealing glimpses of the lake in the distance.

Their ride was mostly silent, which on one level annoyed the hell out of her. He talked to everyone with an easy familiarity—except her.

Maria's stomach dipped and rolled as Dwayne took the turns fast.

"You okay?"

"Car sick."

He paused. She couldn't turn her head to see his expression, she needed to focus on something else.

"You need me to pull over?"

"I'll be fine." She always was.

He said, "Would you rather drive?"

Driving. One more thing she couldn't do *yet*. "No."

"My sister, Teuila, gets car sick."

"Teuila?" she squeaked. "The model?"

"Uh, yeah. You know her?"

"Everyone knows her."

"Well everyone doesn't know that she gets carsick." Dwayne said, "It helps her to be the one driving."

"I don't know how."

Dwayne was silent. "Oh."

Her inadequacies came crushing in on her. The weight of all that she didn't know sat on her lungs, so now she was sick to her stomach *and* couldn't breathe.

Maria stared straight ahead, her fists clenched on her knees, elbows in tight at her sides, holding in the flood of frustration clawing to flow out of her mouth like a river cresting its banks.

In her peripheral vision, his fingers tightened on the wrapped leather wheel. His chest expanded, as if he were about to speak, but she couldn't bear to hear words of pity.

"I was fifteen. I'd only been behind the wheel a few times. Then when I first…got out—" a nice way of saying *escaped my eight years of hell* "—Jack and Bliss and the rest of Stone Consulting were my guards, making sure to keep me safe, so they drove me everywhere, and then I moved to DC and I take the Metro, so—"

"It's no big deal." He rested his fingers over her fist. Once when she was thirteen or fourteen, she'd plugged in a hair dryer and the cord shorted out, zapping her. That was less shocking than the electric buzz from his touch.

Before today, he had never touched her. But since they began this journey, he'd touched her multiple times in a casual, innocuous manner.

The longing she'd suppressed for months roared to life. She yearned so badly for him to touch her in intimate ways. Which would shock the hell out of him.

Maria yanked her hand away.

He huffed a breath as he carefully placed his hand back on the steering wheel. The car was silent again.

"Tell me about your sisters." She needed to do something to break the oppressive silence.

He hesitated. "There are six. You know of Teuila. Sefina is a lawyer, and she'll argue about anything. Samaria is a journalist, freelancing right now, and super nosy. Talia is a fifth-grade teacher, and she has the patience of a saint. Natia is shy and the smartest of us all. She's in med school.

The twins are the youngest. They're eighteen and freshmen in college. La'ei loves fashion and Lulu is all about numbers."

His voice had warmed with affection while he talked about his sisters. It was lovely. He continued on, sharing anecdotes and stories about being the head of the household while they grew up.

By the time Dwayne pulled up to a wrought iron gate with ornate scrollwork, a flurry of flakes had started coming down. The big fat globs splattered the ground and accumulated quickly.

He punched in the security code on the electronic box, and the gate swung open. The long drive led to the lakeshore and revealed a massive sprawling house of timber and stone. Beyond the huge house, Lake Tahoe frothed and swirled.

"This isn't a cabin." Her heart fluttered and her stomach tossed as if she were on the rough waves of the lake. "It's a mansion."

"They do have a big family." Dwayne rubbed the steering wheel as they waited for the gate to open.

Once he parked the Rover in the six-car garage, which was six times bigger than her whole apartment, they entered the house.

"I'll get set up and explore for any protection issues." Dwayne set their bags on the bench in the room off the garage entrance. He spared a quick glance at the racks with skis and the hooks on the wall that held hanging coats and assorted winter paraphernalia.

"I'll help."

"There's no need—"

"I want to learn about how to work in the business," she said stubbornly.

"Okay." He tossed her a pair of snow boots. "Put these on."

Maria slipped off the gorgeous but unsuitable pumps and pushed her feet into the sheepskin-lined boots. She nearly moaned in pleasure.

She followed Dwayne out a side exit and into the yard. The sloping lawn led to a barren dock and deserted beach, currently becoming covered in a thick layer of snow.

The cold seeped into her bones and she shivered.

She'd never seen snow before, but she didn't have time to gaze about in wonder because Dwayne was intent on the security check and if she wanted to learn she needed to pay attention.

"We need to check all the windows and screens. Double check any entrances and all accesses to the house."

They walked the perimeter of the property with Dwayne testing each access point. The snowfall had thickened, coming down with vigor. Maria stepped gingerly through the accumulation.

The house was huge. A wraparound deck extended along the whole back of the house, with French doors at even intervals leading inside the house.

Dwayne knocked on the glass. "Bulletproof."

Maria's eyes widened. Of course she knew Jack's family had money. Anyone who'd been to their house in Monterey would know that, but…bulletproof?

"No window coverings. No way they'd leave their family exposed otherwise."

That made sense.

They continued around the outside, passing a three-story granite chimney and the shuttered windows along the front of the house. Dwayne tested all the downstairs windows and doors before they headed back inside.

After depositing the boots in the mudroom, Maria followed Dwayne down a short hallway, past a small guest bedroom, and reached the huge kitchen filled with a river of granite countertops, shiny white cabinets, and gleaming stainless steel appliances.

Off the kitchen was a vaulted three-story great room that ran almost the entire width of the house with large floor-to-roof windows.

A window over the kitchen sink revealed a view of the storm-tossed waves of Lake Tahoe. In the window, a terracotta pot of herbs scented the air. The cheery plants struck at her, reminding her of her mother and a childhood memory. Her mother had tried to spruce up their rented trailer with cuttings from the fields and forests. In leftover metal coffee cans and soup cans she nurtured the cuttings as if they were the most precious exotic plants. All they needed was love and a bit of water to thrive. Maria had forgotten that about her mother. She thought about her own apartment, barren but for pictures of places she might like to visit one day.

Dwayne's little huff of breath jolted her out of the bittersweet memory.

"What's wrong?"

He glanced out the window, a small frown crinkled the smooth olive skin of his forehead. Maria swallowed the worry that congealed in her throat.

"They may be delayed."

The sky had turned angrier, and the light in the large kitchen had dimmed. His expression, hard to discern, blurred in the darkened atmosphere. The furnace ticked on, releasing a rush of warm air.

The hum nearly drowned out his muttered, "We'll be stuck."

Great. He didn't want to be *stuck* with her.

Not a surprise, and still the sharp words plunged through her heart like a dagger.

Maria turned away from Dwayne, unwilling to show how deep his words cut. She opened the refrigerator door and stared at the groceries lined up neatly inside. She gazed blindly at the contents, hoping he'd go do…something, anything, so he wasn't in the kitchen. With her.

"Maria."

"I think I'll make dinner. How does chicken sound?"

"Maria."

She spied a container of spaghetti sauce on the shelf. "If you aren't a fan of chicken, I can do pasta with red sauce." She spoke desperately over him, hoping he'd go away.

No such luck.

Dwayne put his hand on her shoulder, his palm warm and heavy through the cashmere sweater dress.

Maria froze.

She didn't move, didn't breathe.

"Turn around, please."

She would have resisted but she'd never heard that tone from him. Teasing, yes. Focused at the office, yes. Loving when he'd addressed his mother, yes. But never this tone. Serious and subdued were so far from Dwayne Lameko's normal that she had to find out why.

Maria smoothed out her face, willed away her watery eyes, and closed the refrigerator door carefully. She pivoted, tilted up her chin and looked into his fathomless dark gaze. "Yes?"

"I don't want you to make dinner."

She wasn't going to cower in a corner. She refused to be intimidated, so kept her gaze on Dwayne. "Fine." She stepped to her right.

Dwayne stepped to his left, following her. "I'm sorry."

He was sorry? She stepped to her left, trying again to go around him and get away from his dominating presence. "I don't need your pity."

He stepped to his right, blocking her way again. He loomed over her, but she didn't feel threatened. Caged, anxious to get away from him? Yes. But not scared.

She knew in her soul he wouldn't hurt her.

"You think *pity* is what I feel?" He tipped his head, bringing their faces closer together. So close she was again aware of the flecks of brown and green and gold in his dark eyes.

"No. Yes. I don't know." She'd been lost for eight years. Social cues bewildered her. She had no idea what he was thinking. She only knew she needed to get away from him.

But he appeared oddly hurt.

His broad shoulders blocked the fading light from the window, casting the kitchen in shadows and mystery.

"I would never hurt you."

Not physically. "I know."

As if he couldn't help himself, he cupped her shoulders in his big palms. Maria's breath caught. Held.

He was touching her again.

DWAYNE FROWNED. Maria had tensed beneath his hands.

On the ride from the airport, the scent of her shampoo had swirled in his senses. When she'd stroked the leather seat of the of the Range Rover, he'd started to get an erection, imagining her stroking him intimately. That was never going to happen.

His stomach churned with regret. "Then why are you still so upset?"

Her body language was all wrong. She was stiff, uncomfortable, and he didn't know why. Her shoulders were delicate beneath his much larger palms. "No one touches me."

Shit. He lifted his hands away from her body, fast. "Sorry." Jesus, he'd apologized to her more in the past hour than he'd apologized to anyone in years. He was a "live and let live" guy with solid core values and a confidence in his moral compass.

"No. No." She straightened her shoulders, stared defiantly. "No one touches me."

His heart clenched. No one? He thought about his family. They were always touching. Affectionate. He recalled her stiffness in his mother's arms.

"Why?"

"They're afraid."

Dwayne snorted. She was five feet of nothing with soft curves and a sweet smile. "Of what?"

She shrugged. Looked out the kitchen window over the sink. "I'm a freak," she said softly. "Nature or nurture. Except I didn't have any nurture for…a long time."

"I'm sorry."

She stomped her foot. "Don't be sorry. Talk to me."

How could she throw him so far off his stride? "I am."

"Not like you talk to other…people."

Other people?

"*Women*. Dwayne." Once she let go, she let go. "Other women. You flirt, you tease. But with me, you just…."

Avoid. Of course he did. He wanted her far too much.

What the hell had Jillian been thinking to pair them together on this op? He took an instinctive step back.

"Am I so repellent then?"

What? "It's not you."

She laughed harshly. "C'mon, Dwayne. I might have been in forced solitary confinement for eight years but even I know that's bullshit."

He blinked. He'd never heard her swear before.

"It's not bullshit," he began defensively.

She snorted, that sound of derision goading him. "Right." Her sarcasm hit him in the gut. When she didn't argue, didn't fight back, underscoring the truth that she didn't believe him, something snapped.

"I'm attracted to you." The confession burst out of him with an alarming speed.

Her mouth opened and closed like she was a fish out of water. "What?" she said faintly. A deep burgundy flush spread up her neck and over her face, her eyes sparkling with temper. He'd clearly rendered her speechless.

"You heard me."

Her lashes swept over eyes, hiding her expression. But then she lifted her chin and stepped closer. "Prove it."

Her breasts brushed his pectorals. Shit, he wanted to retreat. Or press against her. Torn in two directions, he stood unmoving in the middle, knowing whatever he decided would change the course of their relationship.

Her long dark curls, streaked with chestnut, cascaded down her back as she tilted temptingly closer. Her body was an artistic map of curves and hollows, with secret tempting places. This close, her clear skin, luminous eyes, and ruby-red lips were like a siren luring him toward the rocks of doom.

Except would it be a disaster if he kissed her?

Dwayne bent his head until their mouths were a sliver apart.

Her warm breath caressed his face as she sighed.

He carefully, gently touched his mouth to hers. Her soft mouth yielded and his eyes drifted closed.

She held stiff against his gentle caress, arms at her sides and her posture awkward. The pillow of her breasts brushed against his pecs as she curled her fingers at his waist. The tentative touch set off mini-detonations inside his skull as she leaned into him, giving him her trust as easily as she gave him the sweetness of her mouth.

He parted his lips, reminding himself to breathe. And in that small opening, she tentatively licked the bow of his upper lip.

The warm, wet contact jolted through him like an electric shock. He sipped at her mouth, keeping the kiss light, not wanting to scare her.

Even as he tried to keep his touch low pressure, desire rampaged his body. His cock rose when she melted against him.

Her rounded belly molded to his hardened erection.

"Oh," she inhaled abruptly, and pulled away.

Dwayne should have apologized but that wasn't him. "Told you."

She flushed a bright embarrassed burgundy. Her gaze skittered to his erection, then away from his body, flitting around the room until landing back on him. That thought that she was probably a virgin blasted through him again. He didn't want to scare her. Even if she seemed willing, she might not realize what she was doing. It was up to him to control and care for her.

He was in uncharted territory right now. Should he continue? Or step back? His body clamored for him to move closer.

Her chest lifted and fell with each hurried gasp but when she swayed toward him, his resolve crumbled.

Dwayne took her hands and guided them to his waist. Her fingertips burned through the cotton of his dress shirt, setting off fireworks throughout his body as he struggled for control.

Dwayne cupped Maria's face in his large palms, holding her carefully as if she were one of his mother's prized ceramic figurines. So precious that his large bumbling fingers might break her if he didn't proceed with care while continuing his slow reverent kisses.

With every sweep of his tongue she pressed closer until they were plastered together. His cock throbbed against her rounded belly. His pecs cradled her breasts. Her neck was canted back at an awkward angle as he increased his easy penetration.

Maria mimicked his actions, her tongue boldly stroking his. She nipped at his lips and their tame kisses gave way to a voracious, intense passion. He dove into the carnal kiss. Lust consumed him as she rubbed her body against his, her moans loud in the cavernous kitchen.

She tugged at him, until her back hit the large door of the Sub-Zero refrigerator. She canted her hips and rubbed against his erection.

Her fingers dug into his shoulders.

She broke away from the kiss. "Please," she whimpered.

Dwayne curled his fingers underneath her generous ass and lifted her easily. He set her on the counter and stepped farther into the V of her legs, the heat of her core burning him. Her fingers burrowed beneath his shirt and slid over the contours of his stomach, her murmur of approval similar to the sound she'd made when she'd stroked the leather seat.

He was harder than the dock pilings as she rocked her softness against him. His fingertips skimmed her bare collarbones, and her breath stuttered.

Dimly he became aware of a phone ringing. The *brrrr-ring* burrowed through his awareness.

"Your cell." The vibration at his waist should have been his first clue, but he'd been lost in Maria.

Dwayne broke away from her, his chest heaving.

Maria pressed her palms to the cool granite countertop. Her gaze snagged on Dwayne and didn't let go.

The old-fashioned ringtone echoed in the empty kitchen as they stared at each other.

Finally Dwayne answered. "'Lo?"

MARIA DUCKED HER HEAD. She couldn't turn away, she was still trapped, his muscled thighs between her hips.

Her body throbbed. Her nipples stabbed the lace of her bra, uncomfortably rubbing the aroused peaks. Her belly clenched. He'd been thick and strong and solid between her legs, his muscled arms holding her tenderly, carefully. Even as he devoured her.

So *that* was passion.

The books she read didn't even come close to describing the sensations he evoked.

Maria licked her lips, tender from the abrasion of their mouths clashing.

"Yeah." Dwayne turned away, rubbing his bald head. His biceps bulged beneath the pressed cotton shirt. All that power—he'd picked her up without even groaning.

But with every passing second that she spent on the cold

countertop, her arousal cooled and embarrassment flooded in.

He was no longer touching her and suddenly those actions taken in the heat of the moment spoke less of passion and more of desperation.

"Uh-huh." Dwayne shot another glance at Maria.

The frigid stone seeped through the thin wool of her dress. Cold assailed her and goose bumps rose as she realized he was perfectly fine while she wasn't sure if she could string together a full sentence.

She shifted on the countertop, and as soon as he took another step back, she hopped off to land solidly on the floor. A sheet of paper fluttered to the tile and she bent to pick it up.

Once her emotions were no longer skimming the clouds, reaction set in. The frantic flutter of her pulse beat between her ears. The rhythm chanted *get out, get out, get out,* and echoed in her head. But his body blocked her exit.

As a distraction she focused on the paper in her hand. The instruction sheet had all the information about the thermostat and electricity if the power went out, which it shouldn't. The backup generator was being delivered next week but chances were they wouldn't need it. Even so, the security system had a separate backup so even if the power did go out they were protected.

Kindling and logs were in the sling by the massive fireplace in the great room. Details blurred together and she lost her focus. Because all those instructions couldn't tell her how to act around Dwayne after their kiss.

Dwayne sighed. "Keep us posted."

He pressed the off button. His beautiful, sensual mouth flattened into a displeased line. "Bitsy and Kita are delayed."

"Well, then I guess I don't need to make dinner." She

tried to step around him, needing desperately to get away from his assessing gaze and her own embarrassed reaction to the wanton way she'd behaved.

"They aren't going to get here until tomorrow morning, at the earliest."

"Well, then I don't need to make breakfast either."

But his words hit with the impact of a solid right hook to her stomach. They were all alone.

For the whole night.

Chapter Eight

Dwayne woke to the sound of absolute silence. After the awkward post-kiss moment in the kitchen, Maria had skittered upstairs and chosen the first bedroom on the right. Dwayne had fixed a plate of lunchmeat and cheese for dinner, and then went over his plan to subtly interrogate Bitsy. All the while he firmly avoided thinking about the kiss.

Bliss and Jack's house was over seven-thousand square feet. Rough-hewn wood beams supported a giant two-story foyer with slate floors. A thick rug decorated the slate floor and a huge chandelier with fake bull horns and tiny shades over pretend candles cast pools of light in the center of the large, basically useless room.

Seven bedrooms, eight baths, a huge kitchen, dining room, and a great room they could hold an Adams-Larsen staff slumber party in and still have plenty of leftover room. He'd double-checked all the doors downstairs, then every door and window upstairs, to be sure they were locked and set the alarm system before falling into bed. Then he had lain there reliving every detail of the mistake.

Hotter than hell.

She might be inexperienced but what she lacked in skill she made up for in sheer enthusiasm. That earnest, sweet fervor killed him.

He hated that she'd run away even if it was likely for the best.

Dwayne had fallen asleep to the constant hum of the furnace. But now the house was dead silent. A ping registered. The security system's backup energy supply had just kicked on.

But the rest of the house remained noiseless.

Dwayne needed to make sure the house was secure. He rolled from the king-size bed and grabbed his weapon from the night table. Before he left the room, he dug through the nightstand and found an unopened box of condoms—holy crap, he did not need to know those were there—and a small halogen flashlight.

His chest was bare but he'd worn a pair of tight long underwear to sleep, in case he needed to be up and about in a hurry. He didn't typically wear anything to bed and the snug material was warm but chafed a bit, especially when he thought about his reluctant and oh-so-sexy partner.

Dwayne flicked on the flashlight and opened the door. The shiny wood floor was cold beneath his bare feet as he stealthily crept down the hallway.

No lights anywhere.

He shot a quick glance out the triangular windows that followed the slant of the ceiling to see if only their house lost power or if the neighborhood was out. But the Stones' cabin was set far enough back from the main road that even if the neighboring houses had had electricity, he couldn't see them.

The furnace was gas but the ignition was electric. So,

once the power shut off, the air inside the house had immediately begun to cool.

Dwayne shivered as he descended the stairs quickly.

He tested the front door. Still locked. He took the first right and headed toward the laundry room near the entrance to the garage.

The breaker box was inside the closet. He flipped open the metal panel and shone the flashlight on the switches. After flipping a few, just to confirm the power loss wasn't just a blown fuse, he concluded that the power was out in the whole house.

He quickly dialed the local power company and confirmed that the area had a blown transformer. Repair crews were being dispatched. Once he discerned there was no threat, he relaxed.

The absolute quiet pressed in on him. His apartment was near a Metro station in a busy area of DC. The hubbub of people and traffic and sounds of the city blended into a background white noise that he took for granted.

But now every sound was magnified, the solemn thud of his heart against his ribcage, the slight buzz of the flashlight, the total quiet more noisy than actual noise. A glow from the great room caught his gaze, then the crackle of wood snapping with fire registered.

Maria had built a fire?

He prowled toward the great room. The slate floor was frigid beneath his bare feet, but he ignored the cold in favor of fanning the flames of his indignation.

"What do you think—" *you're doing?* Maria was sound asleep on the overlarge sectional sofa. Her head rested on a coordinating square pillow in a traditional Native American design, a fleece throw in a deep forest green covered her rumpled pajamas, and an ereader lay face down against her chest. The fire crackled invitingly.

In sleep, her innocence radiated from the gentle slope of her cheeks and the lush curve of her lips. The fall of her silky hair hid her eyes. Damn. His body responded with a ferocious intensity.

Thank God she appeared to be sound asleep.

He dropped into the chair next to the sofa and contemplated the healthy crackling fire. He set his weapon on the side table, turned off the flashlight, and tugged a blanket artfully draped over the back of the chair over his body.

Dwayne propped his chin on his fist and waited for the power to come back on.

The house's backup generator was on the fritz. Bliss had mentioned it in the instruction sheet in the kitchen, but no one had thought the power would go out this early in the winter season. The freak snowstorm was proving them all wrong.

Maria sighed in her sleep, then her legs shifted restlessly. A soft moan escaped her lips. She rolled onto her back, and the sound was louder this time. Her face flushed and her lips parted. And fuck him but she sounded just like she had earlier when she'd been rocking against him and devouring his mouth.

Dwayne's cock rose as her arousal became obvious. The thick stalk pressed against his tight long johns.

He cleared his throat. "Maria," he whispered.

She arched her back, her moans lingering in the cool air.

"Maria." Louder this time, because what else could he do?

Her ereader tumbled to the floor with a thud. Maria shot straight up from her dead sleep. "What?"

Her head swung back and forth, searching for threats, until she realized Dwayne was beside her.

"Dwayne?" The husky rasp of her voice scraped over his nerve endings like the rub of her fingertips on his skin.

"You okay?"

"What are you doing here?" The blanket lost its tenuous hold on her shoulder and fell to her lap, exposing a fire-engine-red flannel pajama top in an old-fashioned cut with lapels and big round buttons.

He was captivated by the delicate shadow between her breasts and the pulse fluttering in the hollow of her throat.

His mouth watered at the thought of pressing his lips to that display of nerves. He swallowed away his desire. "Power is out."

She clutched the blanket to her chest. "Is everything else okay?"

Dwayne averted his gaze from her body and studied the accumulation of snow on the ground and the mounds where landscaping contoured the path down to the beach and dock. Moonlight rippled on the choppy waves of the large, dark lake.

The stillness and the sheer quiet of nature's beauty made it hard to believe anything could be wrong. "The alarm system has its own backup. You're safe."

She stiffened beneath the covering. "Then what are you doing here?"

He stretched so that his bare feet peeped from underneath the fleece. "Keeping warm." He jerked his chin toward the fire. "You do that?"

She nodded.

"Where'd you learn how?"

"I'm not helpless."

"I never said you were." Dwayne hesitated. But he

couldn't bear to sit here and just watch her breathe. He needed her talking, otherwise the temptation of that hollow and his own tenuous restraint wouldn't last long. With the slightest encouragement, he'd be on the sofa continuing what they'd started earlier.

Which would get him in more trouble than he already was. He didn't want to leave the fire—the house was just going to get colder—but he'd noticed the way her gaze dropped to his mouth. She was thinking about their kiss too.

He'd be able to resist his own desires, but if she begged him as sweetly as she had before, he wasn't sure he could resist *her*.

She had one hand in her pocket, clenched in a fist.

"I sometimes watched a survivalist show on television," she answered grudgingly. And he had to backtrack to what he'd asked because his detour into the sensual and pleasurable things he could do to her, that they could do to each other, had fried his brain.

"Good thing, huh?" Her bit of pride made her mysterious eyes sparkle.

Fire skills were not his forte. So, yeah.

"Why were you down here?" Because she'd clearly come to the great room before the power went out.

She stared into the fire. "Couldn't sleep."

"Fooled me," he teased.

"I was reading."

"Oh." He bent to retrieve the ereader that had fallen to the floor. Surprisingly the backlit screen was still on. The illuminated text jumped out at him.

Cock. Lick. Suck.

She leaned toward him, trying to snatch the device out of his hand, but shock had him jerking away from her.

He skimmed the words on the screen. *Sex. Hot. Illicit. Raw.*

His gaze shot to her. "*This* is what you were reading?"

Not that there was anything wrong with reading about sex. But, *but*, this was Maria. And he was pretty sure she was sweet. Innocent. Untried.

Maria had buried her face in her hands. "Kill me now."

The words he read were burned in his brain as he imagined her on her knees, supplicating as she swallowed his cock between her plump lips.

"Holy Mother of God," he whispered reverently.

Shit, he needed to get off this subject. *Get off*—wrong words. His body and brain were still stuck on the image of her on her knees.

His balls were going blue just thinking about denial.

This assignment was going to kill him.

OH MY GOD. Dwayne knew what she'd been reading about. Not that there was anything wrong with reading about sex or romance, but she didn't need him to know in graphic terms what she enjoyed.

She needed to distract him, so she blurted out her true reason for coming downstairs.

"Sometimes when I'm in an unfamiliar place, the walls close in and I need to feel like I'm not trapped." She gestured to the great room with the soaring three-story ceilings with wide open space all around. A massive fireplace and walls of windows brought in the outside. The overwhelming openness of the giant room should have had the opposite effect, but her brain was a strange and wonderful place.

His dark eyes burned with intensity and she averted her gaze.

"Does that happen a lot?"

The embarrassment morphed into an even bigger source of shame. "I don't go many unfamiliar places." Truth.

"Tell me about it."

It. Her ordeal. People typically had two reactions to her forced imprisonment, an unhealthy fascination and wanting to know all the details, or the opposite where they pretended nothing had ever happened to her.

But with Dwayne, neither reaction felt exactly right. He'd asked as if he truly wanted to know. She'd watched him in the office. He was an all-around great guy. Asked about people's lives, knew their idiosyncrasies, everyone loved him and yet, she'd always sensed a distance between him and people as if he didn't want to get too close, using that easygoing cheer to keep people at arm's length.

"You ever talk about it?" he pressed.

No. Even with Dr. Abboud, the **ALIAS** psychiatrist, she'd held back details. "I just want to move on."

"Okay." He propped his elbows on his knees, clasped his hands, and bent over until he was staring at the floor. His bald head gleamed in the warm yellow glow of the fire.

This assignment was a chance to move on. Even if she had sort of fallen into it.

Realization struck. He wasn't trying to get away from her. He wasn't avoiding her. And right now she had a chance to talk to him. Discussing her sex life, or lack thereof, was off-limits but he wanted to know about her kidnapping and imprisonment.

In the flickering light from the burning logs, surrounded

by darkness, and nestled in this safe cocoon, the urge to talk bubbled up.

"I was underground. In a basement of all things. Most houses in California don't have basements."

Dwayne lifted his head, his gaze encouraging, but he didn't speak.

"It was a single room. I had a sofa, a television, a minifridge and a hot plate. And a treadmill. Toilet and sink in a separate corner."

He cleared his throat but didn't speak. Not asking for the salacious details, he let her just talk, which conversely made her want to tell him.

"At first, I thought someone would find me." She laughed and rubbed her biceps through the soft flannel, trying to get warm. "I mean, they had to be looking for me. Right?"

He didn't say a word but he reached out. Curled his fingers around one of her hands and held tight.

"One of the channels the television received had a fitness show on it. I got on that treadmill, I did pushups and sit-ups. I ate my three meals, kept in shape because I knew I needed to be ready to fight."

She sighed, remembering. Each passing day, each hour that no one came, her original conviction that someone would find her, someone would save her, slowly eroded. "But then, no one came to rescue me. It wasn't a sharp break between believing that someone would find me and accepting that no one would ever come." She shook her head. The flannel top gaped open, but to fix it she would have to let go of his hand. And in this moment, his rough palm and his comforting grip were the only things tethering her. "More like a slow erosion of faith."

He reached out his other hand and clasped her palm between his as if he were in prayer.

"I slowed down. Got on the treadmill for an hour instead of an hour and a half. Started skipping meals. Maybe I only did 95 sit-ups instead of a hundred. It was gradual."

She stared at the flames in the fireplace. The heat radiated from the fire but the air around them had chilled. She felt exposed, goose bumps raised, the frigid air licking at her skin like icicles.

"Then one day, I realized I hadn't exercised for a while. My entire existence was lying on that sofa mindlessly watching television. I had lost all hope." Maria shivered, from the memory or from the freezing air, she couldn't say.

But Dwayne noticed. He moved from the chair to the sofa, sitting beside her, shifting her body so that his arms circled her waist loosely and her head rested on his shoulder. While his embrace was relaxed, she sensed that if she tried to move, his arms would tighten to hold her in place.

"What changed?"

"Initially I scratched out the days on the wood coffee table, but I realized that I was running out of room."

She laughed softly.

"It's a wonder I didn't go crazy." Then she shrugged. "Or maybe I did a little."

She was uncomfortable with being touched. She shied away from people when they tried to touch her but in the shadowed warmth of his arms, she relaxed, melted against his chest and let his body shelter hers.

What had changed?

"I was lying there watching television and *The Shawshank Redemption* came on."

His chest stiffened beneath her cheek. "You dug your way out?"

She lifted the hand that Dwayne had been holding, stared at the nicks and cuts that marred her skin. Laughed. "Yes."

"With what?"

"One day I was pacing the perimeter of my room, and I noticed that a spot on the cement wall was crumbling. Just a divot. I had nothing to do so I used the handle of one of my spoons and picked at it. Every day I'd scratch just a little more away."

"How did you hide the hole?"

"Well for one thing, no one ever came down in my prison."

"Then how…."

"They dropped food into the room and used one of those long poles with a grabber to pull up my garbage and waste."

He didn't speak. The warmth from his chest seeped into her back, surrounding her with comfort. "Then when the hole started getting big enough I asked for posters of the woods to put up on the walls," Maria said. "One of the guys who made my weekly delivery felt sorry for me."

She'd worked that. She didn't ask every time but every so often she'd plant a seed of an idea and hope that it took root.

"Once you got through the wall, what happened?"

"Let's just say that the gopher is my favorite animal."

She could feel his confusion. "We were in a drought but the property had gophers. The dirt was hard, definitely harder than the hundred-year-old cement. But I hit a gopher hole and was able to use the animal's burrows. I worked on widening those to get to the surface."

"Why did he put you there instead of…."

"I wasn't supposed to be there the day we were kidnapped. I usually walked to the fields with my friend Ava, but she was sick that day, and so I tagged along with some other girls."

That still didn't explain why she'd been spared from being forced into prostitution.

"At first, we were all in one place." Poor Lucia. "They raped her," she whispered. They'd all heard it. Sometimes Maria couldn't reconcile the sounds she'd heard and the words she read in her romances. But after discussing it with Dr. Abboud, she understood rape was about power and violence not about consensual sex. "They hit her when she wouldn't stop screaming. I think she died from the blow to the head."

He squeezed his arms tighter around her.

The sickness swirled in her stomach. The horror. The fear.

"Fernandez freaked out when he discovered I'd been taken. I had seen too much so he couldn't let me go, but he saved me from prostitution."

She'd been saved from unspeakable horror, and at first, she'd been grateful. So thankful. But then the guilt crept in.

She understood why she'd been spared. "Apparently he had some morals. It was okay to treat Sophia and Graciela as if they were commodities, as if they were just things to be sold, but he couldn't stand the thought of doing that to the daughter of people he knew."

So Fernandez kept her alive and imprisoned, easing his guilty conscience.

"But you got him."

"He's in prison, rotting like he deserves," she said fiercely.

"And the others?"

"The Stones rescued Sophia and Graciela." She'd helped but not as much as she would have liked.

Sadly, she hadn't seen her old friends in a while. They were working at a place that helped rehabilitate former sex-trafficked women. And they were learning to be happy. But they had unresolved anger, and Maria's presence hadn't eased their rage. She couldn't blame them. So they communicated by letter or email, unable to be together in person just yet.

"I will be forever grateful for what Jack and his family did."

"You started it though." He gripped her fingers tightly.

She shrugged. "I guess."

"Those girls would still be trapped if you hadn't rescued yourself."

Sure.

"You are amazing." Dwayne curled his fingers around her hand and lifted it to his lips. He kissed her fingertips one by one. Then he curled his larger palm around hers and pulled her hand against his chest right over his heart.

Warmth flowed through her. The urge to push away from him was strong but the longing to stay cradled in his arms was stronger. She relaxed against him. The hard muscles of his chest were the perfect surface and her body melted against his.

The thud of his heart, the force of the beats, echoed in her ear and against her hand. She'd thought sharing her ordeal would bring back all the emotions and rage and fear that had dominated her existence. But curiously a welcome serenity flooded her.

Chapter Nine

Dwayne woke to a lapful of woman.

Sometime during the night, after she'd fallen asleep in his arms, they had shifted. His head was propped on the arm of the sofa, his legs partially stretched out, with one foot on the floor, the other on the seat cushions. Maria lay on top of him, her head tucked into the curve of his neck, her breasts warm and full against his chest. Her hips were snuggled up next to his and she'd thrown one leg over his thighs.

Her soft cheek rested against the bare skin of his shoulder, and strands of her silky hair brushed his jaw. The easy way she wrapped around him and held him tight would normally have him running for the door. He didn't do relationships.

Except…she felt right.

He didn't have an urge to flee. In fact, if the parts of him that were exposed to the frigid air weren't pebbled with goose bumps, he'd be content to lie here all morning.

The sun was rising over the lake in pink and peach and

purple shades, a glorious display of nature. But clearly the power wasn't back on because it was damn cold.

His morning wood throbbed, her knee close to his balls, and if she shifted at all she'd be up close and personal with his erection.

If he could move without disturbing her, he'd grab his cell and check in with the local power company. Hopefully the electricity would be restored soon. He shifted carefully, not wanting to wake Maria.

But he inadvertently dislodged her, and the first fluttering of awareness came to life as she skimmed her hand over his bare chest. He knew she had to be half asleep because no way would she touch him like this if she were awake.

They might have moved some boundaries, but she was still mostly a cautious stranger. Except hot damn, her callused fingers were toying with his nipple, and his cock got even harder.

Dwayne stifled a groan.

His sharp inhale must have penetrated her consciousness because she came awake with a jolt.

"Oh." She pushed up quickly, but the awkward angle shoved her knee farther up his thighs and she brushed his erection. "Oh."

Her gorgeous burled mahogany eyes widened, and her mouth pursed as she scrambled off him.

"Oh my God." She stood by the sofa now but her gaze was riveted on the bulge beneath his white long johns. And the damn thing grew as she stared.

A flush began in his belly and spread.

He ab curled to sitting and pulled the blanket over his crotch. "Morning." He wasn't about to apologize for being attracted to her.

"Oh, um, good morning." Her toes curled over each other and she wrapped her arms around her waist. The gap in the lapels of the red flannel revealed tempting cleavage.

She glanced around as if searching for a conversational topic that didn't center on his cock.

The moment she saw the vista of Lake Tahoe, her wide-eyed amazement shifted to a different reason. She drifted toward the wall of windows. A pristine white blanket covered the landscape. Trees dripped with icicles and glittered with snow in the early dawn. Mother Nature stunned in her glory.

"It's beautiful."

"Cold. Wet. Slippery."

She shrugged, mesmerized by the shimmering beauty of the fresh snow. "So?"

It occurred to him that this trip might be the first time she'd seen snow.

"It looks so…clean." Simple wonder lit her expression. A shiver shuddered through her. Not the good kind. But he wished it was the good kind. No thinking about sex and Maria.

Dwayne hustled to the fireplace and added logs to the embers, then prodded the wood until the new tinder ignited in a whoosh.

When he turned, she was pressed up against the glass. Her breath steamed the window and her fingers traced the lines of the trees and the lake like a painter stroking a canvas.

The profound longing on her face sparked a deep contrition. "Have you ever played in the snow?"

He knew the answer before she replied.

"No." Her sigh as she turned broke something in him.

"Want to go out in it?" They'd be freezing when they

came back inside but it might be worth it.

"Can we?" Her smile warmed all the bits of ice that congregated in the hollows of his heart. Places he'd frozen on purpose, determined not to open himself up to heartbreak after his father died.

"We can use the parkas and snow gear in the mud room." He was already rethinking the offer but the happiness on her face slayed him. Right now he'd do anything to keep that pleasure from disappearing.

"Really?"

"Sure." Her joy was contagious.

He smiled back and prepared to freeze his balls off.

MARIA HESITATED at the door to the deck.

The world sparkled, the white snow blinding as the sunlight glinted into her eyes. But what struck her was how clean it appeared. Did she want to destroy that picture-perfect scenery?

"What are you waiting for?" Dwayne lifted her with ease and carried her out into the snow. He tromped over the deck and down the stairs to the lawn. He dropped her into the wet mass.

Cold. The damp soaked her jeans immediately freezing her skin. She shrieked at the shock of it.

Oh my God!

But she didn't have time to register the sensations. Dwayne laughed, his face split with a smile as blindingly bright as the snow around them. She'd never seen him so carefree. "It's cold."

He laughed even harder.

She decided screw it. She was going to bring it up. But

in case it made him uncomfortable, she spread her arms wide, tilted her head, and stared at the crystalline blue sky. "I don't think I've ever seen you laugh that hard."

"Couldn't help it. The look on your face was priceless."

"It's cold!"

"I told you it would be."

"You have a lot of experience with snow?" Maria shot him a glance, then twirled around in a dizzying circle. Just like a kid.

"I used to play with my sisters in the winter."

"How old were you?" She stopped breathlessly, her head whirling as she tried to find her balance. Dwayne smiled again and her head spun for an entirely different reason.

"Eighteen."

Not a kid.

"After my dad died, I'd help out my mom. My sisters needed the distraction."

"That's so incredibly—"

"Don't say it." His words were grumpy, even his face had crumpled into a frown.

"—sweet."

"I'm *not* sweet," he growled.

Yet he was. He'd come outside with her even though it was clear that he'd prefer to stay inside and stay warm. Relatively warmer at any rate.

Her head still spun as she stared at the rising sun, light rippling over the placidly calm surface of the lake. He *was* sweet. He loved his mother. Took care of his sisters.

"Get that look off your face."

Maria blinked. "What?" But of course she knew.

She turned away from his knowing look. The boots were too big for her feet but they were keeping them warm. She walked toward the water, kicking her legs up with each stride, flinging the snow in front of her and laughing at the way the fluffy powder shimmered in the frigid air.

"Having fun?" he asked from behind her.

She turned, propped her fists on her hips. "Yes." Being silly in the snow had lightened her mood, which was overshadowed with worry about how he'd treat her after she shared her secrets. She bent and scooped snow and threw it in the air, watching the sparkling flakes sprinkle down like glitter.

"I'd forgotten what fun playing in the snow can be." He grinned again, his smile lighting up the air around them until she could barely breathe.

The feeling of joy spread. Dwayne bent and scooped up a handful of snow. But instead of creating a waterfall, he began packing the snow into a compact ball.

"Oh no." She took off for the protection of the closest giant evergreen, but the ball of snow hit her splat in the back. His laugh came from deep in his belly. With a mini roar, she turned and scooped up her own ball of snow. Even with the mittens, the flakes were *cold*.

She hurled the loose mass with all her might. A portion of the ball disintegrated in midair but the rest hit him in the face because he was bent over laughing so hard.

His shock was priceless. She couldn't help but giggle.

Maria slapped a mittened hand over her mouth.

"I'm gonna get you for that." He scooped up another large handful of snow and charged her.

"No! Don't!" Like he was going to listen to her. Maria was laughing hard as she stumbled toward the tree and safety. Within seconds, he was on her.

Dwayne smashed his large palm full of snow against her face. She shrieked again.

"It's sooooo cold!" Maria gasped. She swiped the snow

onto her mitten and smushed the leftover snow onto his chin and over his smiling mouth.

Dwayne wrapped one arm around her waist, holding her up, then he tenderly wiped the snow from her cheeks. Maria licked her lips and sucked the snow into her mouth.

"You're so pretty," he murmured. His own face dripped with drops of melted snow. "Like an angel."

Suddenly the laughter gave way to intense emotion. A hushed expectation filled the air, the moment fraught with tension as they stared at each other.

The silence was absolute. Even nature stilled around them as if anticipating the break in their control. Wind shushed through the trees, and a large clump of snow fell from one of the branches mere feet from where they stood. But nothing shook his concentration, his entire focus on Maria and her mouth.

His eyes blazed as he lowered his head. Their lips met. Cold. Wet. Perfect.

He kissed her tenderly in soft, tiny caresses. Maria turned so they were pressed together from knee to torso. She twined her arms around his neck, savoring the warmth of his hard body against her softer one.

Dwayne hoisted her up until their mouths were in perfect alignment. In two strides, he had her back pressed up against the large pine tree she'd planned to use for cover.

This time she kissed him. She canted her head, closed her eyes and catalogued each tiny sensation. The rasp of his stubble on her cheek, the tiny bite of his teeth when he scored her lips, the warm stroke of his tongue against hers.

Their kisses became frantic. Breath puffed in the air when he groaned against her mouth. Desire rose in a tidal wave. Her body responded to his kisses, softening and readying.

He rubbed his jean-clad erection against the V in her jeans, their bodies communicating on a physical level. The bulge seemed so big. She'd read a lot of books since she bought her ereader. She knew that women and men fit together during sex but the idea of all that man was intimidating.

And that presumed that he was actually interested.

Sure, he had his tongue down her throat, but he was an equal opportunity dater. Office gossip was pretty clear on that.

Dwayne broke the kiss and dropped his forehead to her shoulder. "What am I doing?"

"If you don't know, then we're in trouble," she replied flippantly, too off balance to worry about revealing that he'd hurt her. Despair knifed her gut in a sharp unexpected slice.

"Shit. I'm sorry."

Maria shoved at his shoulders. "Let me down."

"Maria—"

"It's freezing." She pushed again and he let her slide down his body, dragging the move out slowly so she felt every bulge and muscle on the way. All those awkward moments in the office—when he refused to look at her, when he smiled, not a real smile but a mere tilt of his lips, and then turned away—came rushing back.

She might have wanted him but clearly from the regret on his face, not only were they not not on the same page, they weren't even reading the same book.

"Let's get inside." He tried to grab her hand, but she evaded him by dancing out of his reach.

Maria brushed past him. Now that she wasn't pressed up against her own personal heat source, the cold nipped at her bones and bit at her skin.

Besides the physical cold, her emotions were frozen.

Embarrassment, regret, shame solidified turning her into ice.

She'd been shut down for years. Lost in that prison, she'd subjugated her emotions, refusing to believe in hope. She'd been in an altered state of suspension with no movement.

Now, some days she felt like she was either moving backward or hurtling forward at the speed of sound. And just now she'd hit a wall at a million miles an hour and it fucking hurt.

Maria pounded up the deck stairs and rushed inside.

But the air in the house wasn't much warmer than the outside. The power was still off. She began to shake as the lack of heat radiated outward until she was trembling uncontrollably.

"I didn't mean to hurt you."

She could let him off the hook. "I know."

Suddenly the stilted awkwardness that had infused their interactions at the office was back with a vengeance.

Already she mourned this morning's easy camaraderie. Except now he knew her secrets, knew *her*.

And could use that against her.

Because what she'd forgotten when he was being sweet, and funny, and sexy was that he could also be a total hard ass. His big bulky build wasn't just for show. He was built to enforce, seemed to prefer it, at least at work.

If he wanted to, he could physically crush her with one hand.

As she headed for the shower, she knew her heart was in far more danger than her body. Because the damage he could inflict on her soul was incalculable.

Chapter Ten

The power was back on.

A hot shower had warmed her body temperature back to normal. The thick brown leggings and long, cream wool fisherman sweater was keeping her toasty.

The discontent dogging her was harder to shake off.

Maria assembled the ingredients for chocolate chip cookies on the counter. Laying out the flour, sugars, baking soda, eggs and chips soothed her.

She was still fuming about Dwayne's dismissal. She'd gone over what happened outside while she'd been in the shower and concluded that she might be inexperienced, but she wasn't stupid. He was right there with her until he wasn't. She tried to quell the rage that simmered but instead of petering out, her frustration built.

Screw him.

She closed her eyes, tried to visualize a happy moment. Any happy moment. But she kept recalling how she revealed her inner vulnerability to Dwayne. Now she figured they would go back to awkwardly avoiding each other. Which was going to be rather difficult since they were currently living in the house together and in charge of Bitsy for the next two weeks.

Dwayne sat on the sofa thirty feet away, reviewing the file on Bitsy's stepfather.

"This guy is a real prince," Dwayne said.

Not wanting to talk to him, Maria dug into the cabinet, searching for metal bowls.

"First his lobbyist girlfriend targeted legislation to require all schools carry this specialized nebulizer to combat asthma in kids. Then once that passed, he raised the price of two medicines in the nebulizer by three hundred percent."

Preying on the weak and the fears of parents while he lined his own pockets. Just like José Fernandez had capitalized on the inequitable balance of power in the migrant farmworker community. The parents of the four kidnapped girls had no power. When she and her friends had disappeared, Fernandez had used the crime to raise his profile in the community. He'd been a champion for workers' rights. But the kidnapping had elevated his platform when he exposed how the police had failed to use extra manpower and resources and ultimately failed to find the four missing unimportant girls.

He'd been adored, beloved in the community, rising through political ranks until he'd been on the cusp of being appointed Secretary of Labor by the President of the United States.

Until Maria had escaped and revealed his horrible deeds. That *he* had been the man behind the kidnappings. All for personal gain.

"Bastard." She spit out.

"No argument here."

"Her stepfather deserves to go to prison."

Fernandez was in prison. His brothers, the actual kidnappers, were in prison too. Away. Where they could no longer hurt her friends. Justice was served. But too late for Maria and her parents. Maria fingered the rosary beads wrapped around her wrist. A peculiar sorrow invaded her.

She would like to see her mother, although according to the facility where her mama resided now, she likely wouldn't even know who Maria was. Since her escape, her mother's condition had gone downhill. Almost as if now that Maria was safe, she could let go.

"He does. I hope that Vandenbeek's crimes and misdeeds come to light." Dwayne shifted his focus to his laptop. "No one should ever put a child at risk."

"Bitsy will do good to be free of him," Maria continued. "Assuming ALIAS relocates her."

"Why didn't *you* take Jill and Marsh's offer?" Dwayne continued to click through the documents on his laptop.

"You knew about that?" Her boss had offered to relocate her. Had offered to give her a new life. But Maria had chosen to live the life she had. She'd refused to let Fernandez win. She hadn't wanted to be afraid anymore but deciding not to be afraid and actually accomplishing it were two different things.

Maria opened the door between the refrigerator and the hallway to avoid looking at Dwayne. Inside the well-stocked pantry, a shiny new KitchenAid mixer sat on a shelf. The expensive appliance didn't look like it had ever been used.

Heavy. She carefully removed the stand mixer from the shelf and set it on the counter reverently. Her fingers skimmed over the shiny red enamel. The KitchenAid was the ultimate for home cooks and bakers. Her handheld beaters, picked up at the local thrift store, were not even in the same stratosphere.

One day….

"What'cha making?"

Maria jumped.

Dwayne's breath was hot on her neck. How had he managed to sneak up on her?

"Chocolate chip cookies."

"Yum." He rubbed his flat stomach and she wanted to punch him all over again.

Even though she walked on the treadmill daily, her penchant for homemade baked goods was evident in her rounded belly.

She didn't want him in here, trying to be nice. The kitchen was her refuge. "Get out," she managed politely and calmly, without the stabby that wanted to emerge.

"Why?" He curled his fingers around her arm, his light hold chaining her to the floor as if he'd shackled her with iron.

Maria tried to shrug off his hand, but he wasn't budging. She kept silent. Besides, what was there to say? The man who would sleep with anyone—okay, maybe that was a slight exaggeration—wasn't interested in her.

It shouldn't hurt. But it did.

Before Dwayne could press for an answer, his phone pinged, telling him he had a text.

He let go of her and frowned at the screen. "Kita and Bitsy will be here soon."

Maria nodded and began measuring the dry ingredients. With brisk efficiency, she whipped up the dough. Running her palm over the matte finish of the stainless steel double ovens, she sighed in jealousy.

"What?"

She waved her hand to encompass the entire room. "So gorgeous." She didn't have much use for *things*. But even she could admit that this kitchen was a fantasy room. More counter space than her entire apartment. Multi-colored granite with thick rounded edges and stainless steel prep sinks gleamed with barely a scratch. Two double ovens appeared to barely be used. Two dishwashers. And a generous-sized pantry with plenty of storage. They even had a warmer.

Dwayne turned in a circle. Shrugged. "It's nice."

Nice?

Maria scooped the balls of dough onto a brand new cookie sheet, then slid the first batch into the oven while Dwayne headed for the garage to get ready to welcome Bitsy and Kita.

Maria prepped to spread the warm baked cookies on paper towels.

A bit later, Bitsy and Kita hustled into the kitchen. Dwayne followed behind, lugging four matching fuchsia suitcases of varying sizes. He gave her a chin lift and headed up the stairs.

Clad in a pair of blue jeans, stiletto ankle boots, and an oversized cashmere sweater with an asymmetrical cowl neck, Bitsy could have stepped out of *Town and Country* magazine.

"Cookies!" Kita clapped.

Bitsy Vandenbeek plopped her borderline-too-thin figure onto the stool at the giant pool of granite island. "Cookies?"

Maria slid two gooey warm cookies onto a paper napkin and handed them to Kita, then did the same for Bitsy and for herself.

Maria savored a bite of a cookie, the melted chocolate

bitter and sweet against her tongue. She closed her eyes, enjoying the treat.

"You aren't going to eat another one, are you?" Bitsy's strident voice broke into Maria's enjoyment. Her eyes popped open as Kita shoved a second cookie into her mouth.

"Hell, yes." Kita licked her fingers. "So good."

Maria nibbled on her cookie.

"The calories in one of these will add ten pounds in no time." Bitsy pushed the napkin away after taking one bite. "Willpower is imperative."

The sweetness soured on her tongue at Bitsy's snide comment.

Dwayne sauntered into the kitchen as the timer went off. He snatched a cookie from the cooling batch on the counter.

Maria set her cookie on the napkin, her appetite gone.

"Chocolate chip cookies are the ultimate comfort food," Dwayne chastised. "You should be thanking her."

Bitsy sniffed.

While the support was unnecessary, his words spread like the melted gooey chips. She wasn't about to let Bitsy food shame her.

"After eating the same thing week after week, being able to bake homemade chocolate chip cookies is a luxury I will never deny myself the pleasure of or take for granted."

Bitsy said, "Oh."

Maria couldn't tell if the exclamation was surprise or apology and she didn't care.

"Maria makes the best cookies on the planet," Kita boasted.

"That's because they're clearly baked with joy," Dwayne said. "My mama always says food prepared with love tastes better."

Her heart melted. "That's beautiful."

Dwayne's smile tipped her emotions toward affection. She was on a seesaw—happy, then angry, then happy again —like the rusted old playground equipment in the park near her childhood trailer.

Bitsy huffed out a breath. "They won't taste so good when your looks are gone and you've got nothing left to barter."

All three of them stopped. Stared at Bitsy.

"What?" Their client stared longingly at the cookie. "It's true."

"Looks aren't everything," Dwayne said.

"Spoken like a man." Bitsy rolled her eyes.

Maria shook her head, not willing to let this pass. "My body, my life."

A crinkle appeared between Bitsy's brows, as if she truly couldn't understand Maria's reasoning, and she opened her mouth, ready to argue.

"Kita, heard you're moving in with the Fed." Dwayne effectively shifted the conversation.

Kita straight-up blushed. *Blushed.* "Ah, yeah."

It was sweet, it was unexpected. The kick-butt-self-defense expert was smitten.

"The badass is blushing." Dwayne's smile spread. "Let me know if he doesn't treat you right and you need me to beat him up for you."

"I can put my own hurt on," Kita taunted, but her sparkling eyes betrayed the truth.

Even as her happiness for Kita expanded, Maria's ire rose at the easy affection in Dwayne's voice. He never talked to her that way. Except for those stolen moments on the sofa and in the snow, he treated her like a pariah.

"Can I go freshen up?" Bitsy interrupted the moment.

"Not yet. We've got some logistics to go over." Kita gestured to the sectional. "Have a seat and we'll get started."

Maria baked cookies while Kita went over Twitter and Instagram, showing her what they were going to post and explaining the logic behind each one. Pictures of Bitsy in New York. An Insta of her wrapped in a towel with a mask on her face. "The most important thing for you to remember is that you can't post anything. These are designed to mislead anyone who is looking for you."

"I'm not stupid, I get it."

Her defensive tone and the uncertainty in her voice made Maria pause. She'd learned a thing or two over the past year. Bitsy didn't believe what she was saying. Maria was moving before she even realized what she was going to do, because underneath that spoiled aggression, there was hurt.

Kita said, "I never said you were stupid."

Maria placed her palm on Bitsy's shoulder. "Kita just wants to reiterate so you don't forget how important it is not to reveal your location."

"Yeah, fine. I get it." Bitsy shrugged off Maria's comfort.

"And here's the last one, post spa." Kita pointed at the pic of Bitsy with a glowing face and a handful of shopping bags.

Bitsy stared at the photo. "That's what I'm good at. Looking pretty and spending money."

Dwayne had stayed mostly silent during the past half hour, pretending to read on his laptop but observing Bitsy. He might have fooled everyone else, but Maria had noted that he'd kept close attention on their client and not whatever was on his computer.

"On that note, I'm out." Kita wrapped several cookies in a paper towel. "I've got to get back to DC."

Dwayne bent and brushed Kita's cheek with a kiss. Unexpected emotion twisted Maria's stomach again. She had no reason to be jealous, and yet that simple affectionate caress made her want to growl like the black bears Tahoe was known for.

Kita squeezed Dwayne then stepped back. "Maria, see me out?"

"Sure." Maria shook off the odd jealousy and directed Dwayne, "Take that last batch of cookies out of the oven when the timer goes off."

Dwayne was giving Maria and Kita a look that easily communicated, "Don't leave me alone with her!" But they ignored him.

Maria walked with Kita to the garage.

"Watch that one." Kita frowned toward the great room.

"What?" Just because Bitsy wouldn't eat cookies wasn't a reason to be suspicious.

"I don't know. But I trust my gut and my gut is saying, watch out."

Maria shook her head. "She's misunderstood."

"She's trouble." Kita hefted a backpack on her shoulder. "So, if you need to talk about anything, you know you can call me. Right?"

She was confused. "You think I'll need to talk to you about Bitsy?"

"Not her. Him."

"Dwayne?"

"Sparks are flying."

Maria flushed.

"You like him!"

Maria opened the door to the garage where Kita had parked a small compact car. "Don't you need to be leaving?"

"Taking the hint." Kita patted her on the arm. "Bliss and Jack are only a few hours away if you need them."

"I know."

"Hopefully you won't."

Part of Maria would love to see her friends again, but with them came the old expectations and limitations. One of the reasons she'd moved away from California was to escape the stifling concern of her friends. Dwayne would never see her as a competent woman if they were around.

She didn't need help. "I'll be fine."

<hr>

MARIA WAS BACK in the kitchen.

Something in her face, her body language, had Dwayne's instincts going on alert. "Everything okay?"

"Why wouldn't it be?" Maria busied herself with putting the cookies into a whimsical ceramic cookie jar in the shape of a castle.

Okay he wasn't touching that with a ten-foot pole. Instead he focused on Bitsy, who'd gotten up off the sofa and wandered into the kitchen.

"How you doing?"

"Bored."

She just got here. How could she be bored already?

She grabbed Maria's hand. Only a blind person might miss how much Maria tensed, but she reluctantly let Bitsy lead her to the sectional sofa.

She threw her body onto to the sofa, right over the spot where he and Maria had slept.

This spoiled socialite lounging on the place where they connected irritated him on a subliminal level.

Even more telling was Maria's hesitation before sitting

down in the corner, nowhere near the site of their unexpected intimacy. He couldn't help but feel it was a rejection of him.

"So." Bitsy rubbed her hands together. "Give me the 4-1-1."

Maria jerked. "Um. Sure. I guess we can do that."

"What did you do for eight years?" Bitsy's eyes were bright with an avaricious curiosity.

Irritation caromed through him. What the fuck?

Maria said, "I'm sorry?"

Bitsy's smile was almost gleeful. "It must have been crazy boring."

"That's one way of putting it."

His temper simmered. Bitsy had zero sensitivity. Dwayne edged closer, ready to catch Maria if she stumbled, figuratively of course.

"You were what? Fifteen?" Bitsy laughed, but there was a wistful quality to the sound. "What a drag. Missing the parties, missing all the normal stuff that teenagers get into. When I was that age I was stealing my stepfather's Porsche and joyriding around Virginia, shoplifting from Bergdorf's, having sex in my boyfriend's pool house." She sighed, oblivious to the fact that Dwayne was about to take her head off. Of all the fucking insensitive, idiotic things to say. "Life was so much simpler then."

Dwayne took a step toward Bitsy. But before he could say a word, Maria jumped to her feet. "You think that's what I missed?" Her rich burled eyes sparked, her arms flying wildly, and her voice quavered. But he couldn't tell if it was from temper or because she was upset.

"Well, sure. I mean, I would have gone crazy if I hadn't been able to rebel."

Maria stabbed her finger at Bitsy. "I missed my friends,

one who was raped and murdered in the next room. I missed my parents, who had no idea what happened to me and no real recourse because I was just a poor Mexican girl who no one cared about. I missed human interaction. I missed my fucking cat. I missed my mother's carnitas and my abuela singing me to sleep at night."

Bitsy's mouth was hanging open. Her perfect white teeth snapped together. "Well. Sorry." But she didn't sound sorry.

"I fucking missed my life." Maria began to pace. "You want to know what it was like? It sucked."

Bitsy's eyes widened. And Dwayne couldn't help but think that Maria was selling Bitsy on the idea of going back to DC and reclaiming her life. If she kept it up, he wouldn't need to convince Bitsy. Maria would do it for him.

"My companionship was a television that got three channels, in English, which was my second language back then. I lost everything in an instant and it will never be the same. And you have *no right* to interrogate me."

Maria's chest heaved. Tears trembled on her thick lashes but didn't fall. Because she was magnificent. Strong. Powerful. A goddess who rose above her trials and triumphed.

Bitsy did a head shake. "Well, I was just asking." She stood quickly and looked at Dwayne. When she gave him an eye roll he wanted to boot her out so badly, he nearly bit his tongue. "I'm going to my room."

Bitsy stared at Maria, the hunch in her shoulders transmitting her dejection. Then she snapped her shoulders back and said defiantly, "You realize you'd never be here right now if it hadn't happened? Look around. You'd never have been exposed to all of this if you'd grown up the way you were supposed to."

Dwayne shifted his attention to Maria. Her sadness was easy to see.

Bitsy's insight was true, and yet Bitsy was missing the point. Maria didn't care about stuff or this house or even her job. She just wanted human interaction. To be touched.

The way he had touched her yesterday.

But he couldn't be the one to give her that comfort. Because he knew without a doubt that touching would lead to intimacy, and he couldn't afford to add to his list of responsibilities.

Incomprehensible that Bitsy was the one who'd hammered that point home to Dwayne, but there it was.

Bitsy stomped away in a huff.

Maria faced the wall of windows and stared out at the gorgeous day. Her arms were wrapped tightly around her waist, and her misery was reflected in the glass. "I'm sorry."

What? "Why?"

"I should never have yelled at our client." Maria pressed her palm against the glass. "She's our responsibility and I totally lost my temper."

He took a step toward her. Paused.

"You were much easier on her than I would have been." Dwayne wanted to fold her in his arms and hold on tight. "I was two seconds from jumping all over her ass," he confessed. "But you beat me to it."

"I let my temper get the best of me." The anguish in her voice clinched it.

Even if he didn't want additional obligations, he also couldn't let her suffer. Her words reverberated in his brain and he gave in to his need to comfort her. Or maybe he was comforting himself.

Dwayne stepped up behind her and wrapped his arms

around her shoulders. He rested his chin on her hair. "You wouldn't be human if that conversation didn't upset you."

She breathed in deep, held it.

He savored the temptation of her in his arms. Her soft body held rigid against his embrace, but she didn't shove him away. He sensed that she needed this contact as much as he did.

She swiped angrily at her tears. "But still. I'm supposed to be getting better. Sometimes this anger just chains me up until I can't see straight."

"What happened to your friends?"

"What?" she sniffled.

"Your other friends."

He realized he'd been so busy trying to keep his distance from her, trying to deny the attraction and keep her safe from him, that he hadn't been asking the right questions.

One girl had died. Maria now worked in DC. But where were her other two friends? He knew they'd been found. After she'd escaped her prison, the Stone family had made it their mission to find those girls. And they'd done it.

"They're at a farm that specializes in rehabilitation and a safe place for women who've been trafficked." She straightened her shoulders. "Which is why we've got to make sure we keep Bitsy happy."

Dwayne frowned wishing she would lean back against him again. "You lost me."

"If we end up converting Bitsy to a long-term client, a portion of her fee will go to the organization, S.S.A.F.E. It stands for Security, Shelter, and Freedom for the Exploited."

"How do you know that?"

"Because I handle the donations. And every time we have a relocation, Adams-Larsen donates a portion of the fee to them."

Fuck.

Dwayne was supposed to be convincing Bitsy not to disappear but to go back and legally testify against her stepfather. The Justice Department was building a case against the jerk now.

Maria would hate him if he succeeded.

Chapter Eleven

The rest of the day passed without incident. They had retreated to their own corners. Maria finished her book and, to keep herself busy, made dinner. It was nice to cook for other people. That was why she liked to bake. She could share her treats with everyone in the office.

The rich pork chops in an apple and gorgonzola sauce were easy to whip up. Of course, Bitsy ate only salad with a drizzle of dressing. Her insistence about staying thin had struck a chord with Maria. Life was too short not to enjoy it.

Bitsy seemed so concerned with her looks but her words felt parroted rather than something she truly believed. "Got to keep up my public image. Vandenbeek's have a certain standard to uphold."

The atmosphere at dinner had been tense.

Bitsy sulked. Dwayne had been pensive. And Maria had just wondered if somehow she was responsible for everything wrong.

When dinner was over, Bitsy went to bed, leaving Dwayne and Maria alone.

Maria was antsy and horny, and she needed to finish

cleaning up. Dwayne offered to help, and the concept was foreign enough that she hadn't had the foresight to say no thank you. Silently, they cleared the table, and now they were scraping dishes and loading the dishwasher like an old married couple.

He'd said earlier that her outburst at Bitsy was okay but his actions now were confusing her. Had he lied about her loss of control being okay or had he changed his mind?

Dwayne cleared his throat. "Thanks again for dinner."

"It's nice to cook for someone else." And didn't that sound pathetic?

"It was amazing." Dwayne smiled. "I pretty much buy premade salads and steam chicken breasts except for Sunday dinners with my family."

"I can…share the recipe if you'd like."

She stood between the large island and the sink while Dwayne was across the sea of granite.

"That would be great."

The stilted conversation between them hurt. She missed the easy camaraderie that they shared outside during the fun in the snow. Once Bitsy arrived, the ease between them had disintegrated.

She wanted that casual, simple affection back. Except nothing between them was simple.

Nothing *for her* was simple.

Most days she accepted that when her life had paused for an inordinate amount of time, much of her development had been stunted. She might never recover from her ordeal but still she fought to try. Being here, taking on this assignment was a step in the right direction.

Dwayne moved until he was next to her at the sink. His presence intimidating, yet not. His bulk was huge but instead of making her fearful, his broad shoulders, massive chest, and thick thighs made her feel protected, petite, like nothing could get through him to her.

While she logically knew it was an illusion, she liked it.

The heat emanating from his body enveloped her—warming her and awakening feminine places, making her long for the intimacy she read about.

They reached for the same pan, their fingers tangling in the warm soapy water.

His hand was so much bigger than hers. Just like that, her mind went to the bulge she'd seen. To the book she'd been reading when he'd picked up her ereader…and the words he'd seen if his blush was anything to go by. The fact that he could blush was a revelation.

Wasn't he the free and easy guy in the office? He wasn't a total slut, not that she had any issue with that, but shouldn't he be comfortable with sexual freedom?

Yet, he had blushed.

The sip of wine—Bitsy had insisted they needed wine with their dinner—had long since worn off, but perhaps she could ask under the guise of being tipsy.

Maria's half glass sat on the gleaming granite counter. Dwayne hadn't had any because he was their muscle. But maybe he hadn't been paying attention to how much she'd had to drink.

The empty bottle indicated that Bitsy was likely drunk. Her misery at being stuck in a remote Tahoe house had been communicated loudly and often.

Maria leaned closer. Maybe his kisses outside, or Kita's insistence that Dwayne was attracted to her, made her bold but she wanted to know. *You never get what you don't ask for.*

She read that somewhere.

But she couldn't just…blurt out the request. Could she?

Dwayne had just taken a sip of water when the plea came out like a big pile of word vomit.

"Have sex with me?"

He choked, started coughing so hard, she had to slap him on the back. "What?" he wheezed.

Too needy. Damn.

No way was she saying it again. "You heard me."

"I can't if you're innocent—"

"I haven't been innocent since I heard my friend get raped." *He can't if I'm innocent? What kind of excuse was that?* "I'm inexperienced. There's a difference."

"That's what I thought." But he looked away, turned his body, so her view was of his shoulder. "You need to wait until it's special."

"Why aren't you special?"

He sputtered. "Because I won't stick around."

"I didn't ask you to." In her life, no one stuck. Perhaps it wasn't fair but she'd been abandoned by pretty much everyone. "I have no expectations about people staying."

The statement was bald. Uncompromising.

He must have sensed her earnestness.

"Maria…."

"If you don't want to, don't lie. Just say no."

"No."

Wow, after last night and today in the snow, she hadn't quite expected that. Her confidence deflated like a popped balloon.

"Fuck. No, that's not true." Dwayne bent his head and rubbed his big palm on the back of his neck. "Of course, I want you."

She snorted. "Yeah, you're bowling me over with your lust."

"I don't want you to regret anything."

"Are you not any good?" She didn't see how that was possible but weirder things had happened to her, so, yeah.

He choked again. "What? Of course not. I mean, I'm good. Shit." He was flustered enough that she laughed. Apparently questioning his sexual prowess was the way to throw him off balance. "I mean, I've never had any complaints."

But he moved further away from her, not closer.

"Okay." She wasn't sure what to do next. "Let's do it."

He choked again.

Maria sighed. "Frankly, you're not reacting the way I thought you would."

"You're not acting the way I thought you would either, so we're even."

Now that she'd thrown it out there, she'd hoped he would take the reins and make this happen but, true to the way her life unfolded, even trying to have sex wasn't easy.

"In the books I've read, the guy usually jumps on the girl when she says let's have sex."

He chuckled. "But this is your life. I don't want you to regret anything."

"I regret that I was in stasis for eight years." Frustration welled. She knew he wasn't trying to be difficult but at the same time, she just wanted to break down this barrier. She escaped her captivity but she was still stuck. "I'm still trapped. And I don't have time for regrets. I used up that time when I was a prisoner."

"What about a…compromise?"

A compromise? She pulled the stopper and the water drained from the sink. Instead of looking at him, she watched the water circle the drain like her hopes disappearing.

"What if we…play a little?"

Play? "I'm not sure I know how to play." The words were sad, true.

"I could teach you." Dwayne studied her. "You're sure?"

"You're giving me a complex, Lameko." Maria slapped the dishcloth into the sink. "I know I'm no skinny Bitsy but I'm not a troll either."

"Hey." Dwayne turned her so she faced him head on. With his index finger he tilted her chin up until she was staring into his dark gaze. "Don't talk like that. You're gorgeous."

"Yeah. That's coming through. You don't have to feed me lies, just…do things to me." She was sure other women didn't have to beg men to have sex with them. Was it always this hard?

"I'm ignoring that you think I'm lying—" his grin lit up the room, his cheeks creased and his eyes sparkled "—in favor of doing *things*."

Thank goodness.

***

DWAYNE HAD no idea what he was doing.

But Jesus, he had dreamed of this for months. He sought out one-night stands in order to forget her. But nothing worked.

Now she was in his arms. He was going to do all the things he'd fantasized about and he would be the best *almost* lover she'd ever have. He had no intention of squandering the opportunity.

But he knew one thing, he wasn't going to expose Maria to scrutiny so they needed a neutral, private location away from Bitsy.

The guest bedroom off the kitchen was perfect. The

security alarm was set. Bitsy was decently drunk when she went to bed. Even so, if she tried to escape she'd need a car or access to the garage to get the gate open, and he'd be able to stop her quickly.

He grabbed Maria's hand, her fingers soft and pliant in his. "How about we start here?"

Dwayne wouldn't take her innocence but hopefully he could give her an experience to remember.

Before this mission, his attraction to Maria had been mostly physical with a dash of admiration for her guts thrown in. But she'd been afraid of him and he hadn't wanted to scare her. Now that he'd gotten to know her, he liked her. She was smart, funny, and full of joy. So it was imperative that he not take something precious, something she could never get back.

He led her toward the guest bedroom.

No hesitation in her step, no worry clouded her beautiful burled mahogany eyes. Her features had lightened as if he'd given her a gift.

Once they were inside the room, Dwayne paused, hesitated. He couldn't claim they got carried away. This was a deliberate move toward physical intimacy.

"I just want to make sure—"

Maria closed the door with a quiet snap. "I'm sure."

The bland room consisted of a closet, a dresser, a nightstand, and a bed. The large queen size bed with lots of pillows and flannel sheets had plenty of room for them to play. Before he could say another word, she pressed her palms over his pectorals. His heart thudded in triple time beneath her warm fingers as she pushed him toward the bed.

He let her. "What do you think you're doing?"

"Compromising?" She smirked as she reached for his belt buckle.

"Not yet." He grabbed her fingers and tugged her hands behind her back, pulling her body into his, taking her weight and savoring the cushion of her breasts against his hard chest.

All those times he'd watched her in the office, bumbling around her like a guy who couldn't find his dick if he had a map, he'd suppressed the heat she'd generated in him. But he'd fantasized about having her, so he knew exactly how he wanted to touch her. Hold her.

"But—"

Before she could argue, he pressed his lips to hers.

Soft. She was so soft and eager.

Her mouth opened beneath his, and she stroked her tongue along his.

He didn't want to scare her. Dwayne slowly backed toward the bed and when his knees hit the mattress, he fell back, taking her with him.

He let her hands go and she wrapped her arms around his neck and held on as they tumbled to the bed.

Dwayne groaned as she landed in the V of his legs.

Maria broke their kiss and pushed up. The move fitted her sex against his growing erection. "Did I hurt you?"

Dwayne slid his palms underneath her sweater along her ribs, marveling at how soft her skin was. "You couldn't hurt me if you tried." At least…not physically. Emotionally, when it came to Maria, he seemed to waffle between wanting to keep his distance, the smart choice, and needing to be closer to her, to understand her, to explore what made her tick. That choice spelled disaster.

She blinked, then her lids lowered as he skimmed his fingers along the sides of her breasts. Her round fullness would overflow his hands, he tingled with the need to squeeze and pluck but he wanted to proceed cautiously.

Dwayne rubbed his thumbs over her distended nipples in leisurely circles. Her breath caught, held as he supported the weight of her upper body with his hands.

Her eyelids fluttered shut.

He didn't even think she was aware of her movements, but her hips rocked in time to his small caresses, rubbing against his cock through his jeans.

Maria licked her lips and arched her back, pressing her breasts into his hands. Her body moved faster. She was so fucking responsive. They hadn't taken any clothes off and she was making erotic noises that sparked his own growing arousal.

Dwayne used his thumbs to scoop inside the lace cups of her bra and apply pressure to her tight nipples.

"Oh." Her eyes flew open, and desire shimmered in the brown depths.

God, he needed to see her.

Dwayne shoved her sweater up and over her head. Maria propped on her knees to help him get the wool top off. He tossed it to the floor.

He held her aloft, his palms spanned her ribs as she lifted until his mouth could reach her nipple. Her aureoles puckered, the sweet cherries of her nipples begging for him.

His mouth watered. He tongued a tight bud. Her gasp was like a match to kerosene, and he couldn't stand it any longer. "So sweet." He squeezed her breast and tugged her nipple into his mouth, rolled it against his tongue and then closed his lips over her flesh and sucked. With his fingers, he plucked at her other nipple.

Maria straddled his thighs, her thin leggings a small barrier to the heat of her sex. She rubbed her hot core against him. His erection pressed against his zipper so hard he'd have ridges. Her hands were clenched on the fabric at his shoulders, her entire body engaged in the simple foreplay.

The dark flush of desire reddened her skin and brightened her eyes. The light from the ceiling created a halo around her head, casting her in an angelic glow.

"*Dios mío*," she cried.

Dwayne sucked harder and rocked his painful erection against her covered mound. The sounds she was making were going to kill him. The muffled groans and soft sighs ramped his arousal higher.

She arched, head thrown back, eyes closed. Her lips were plump and shiny, her breasts flushed, and nipples begged for his mouth again.

Dwayne continued to play her body, working to wring every moment of pleasure out of her first orgasm of the night.

She was close. Her mouth dropped open as she gasped for air. She threw back her head and her thighs trembled around his hips. With a cry, her body shook when she shattered.

Satisfaction roared through him. He wanted to howl and thump his chest with achievement, as if he'd made the winning touchdown instead of delivering a dry hump.

The need to connect, to penetrate her was primal. He slid one hand along her back and cupped her neck. Threading his fingers through her silky hair, Dwayne tugged her head down so she met his mouth in an unfettered kiss.

"One down." He licked at her lips, needing to tell her how beautiful that orgasm was. Wondering why the hell he'd ever resisted. "Number two coming up."

Maria blinked, giggled. "Two?"

"To start." Dwayne shoved at her leggings, needing her bare. "I need to touch you."

"Anything." She nipped at his mouth even as he tossed her leggings. "Yes. Good." Each word punctuated with a kiss. "Please."

God, he'd taken her panties with the leggings, and his hands were full of soft, round gorgeous ass.

Her legs straddled his thighs and he squeezed her butt, needing to taste her. He slid his fingers along her sex, and the slick folds welcomed him. He rubbed, spreading her juices, and thought his fucking cock would explode. But that wasn't going to happen.

She needed to know she could trust him. Playing only.

Playing might kill him.

Chapter Twelve

Maria's head spun.

Dwayne rolled them on the bed so that she was beneath him. He threaded his fingers with hers and pressed her hands to the mattress next to her head. His weight anchored her to the bed. It should have been suffocating but his bulk felt like a shield.

Like he would protect her from whatever came her way.

Her body was limp, replete. Tiny aftershocks sizzled through her and her heart continued to beat at a frenetic pace.

She couldn't believe she was here. In bed with Dwayne.

She'd dreamed of this for months. Wanted him on a visceral level that defied logic.

The orgasm had been wonderful, mind blowing, epic. But she wanted to touch him too. His face was a mask of concentration and hard lines, and his dark eyes glittered with a primal satisfaction. His cheeks were flushed and his lips reddened as his gaze scanned her body.

His erection, so thick and big, throbbed against her.

Her nipples tightened, wet from his mouth and exposed to the cooler air.

"Let me touch you," she begged.

Dwayne released her hands, and excitement fluttered through her. He lifted his hips and, hovering over her on all fours, unsnapped her bra and spread the cups wide. He trailed his tongue over her body, tasting her flesh, sipping at her skin, as she eagerly undid the buttons on his shirt.

The act seemed unbearably intimate in the silent cave of this room.

When she got all the buttons undone and parted his shirt, there was another T-shirt underneath.

Maria shoved the flannel shirt off his shoulders and down his arms. His biceps were so big. Bigger than her thighs and yet he was so gentle when he touched her.

His fingertips trilled over her breasts like a concert pianist caressing the keys; he played her body, strumming her nipples, fluttering his fingers against her stomach and lower.

Underneath his flannel was a plain white T-shirt. She pushed the soft cotton up, tugging ineffectually until he reached behind his neck and pulled the shirt off one-handed. Finally he was as exposed as she was.

His olive skin gleamed in the low light, smooth and sleek and layered with muscle. He was hot, burning up under her hands. His muscles bunched as he skimmed his mouth over rounded stomach, nipping a path to her sex.

Her legs twitched restlessly as he kissed lower. Slow kisses that set off tiny detonations beneath her skin. She trembled on the edge as his destination became clear. "But it's my turn to touch you."

She grasped for his shoulders but he was out of her reach. With his thumbs he traced a line from her belly button down to her pubic bone, stopping just before he reached the sensitive bud of her clitoris. Her stomach contracted at the light touch. He licked the sensitive skin of her belly with hot, wet openmouthed kisses, moving closer to her sex.

She'd read about this. Wondered how having a man kiss her *there* could possibly be all that exciting. Honestly it had sounded sort of disgusting. But she didn't want to miss out on anything. She quivered with anticipation as he moved lower.

Then she felt him. An intimate kiss, his tongue on her folds.

"Oh!"

He peered up at her, the lower half of his face hidden by her dark curls, his eyes bright. "Okay?"

"Yeah." Her voice breathy. She cleared her throat. "Yes, please."

He smiled, his cheeks pressed against her inner thighs. "Okay then."

Dwayne slid his arms beneath her thighs, until her legs rested on his huge arms. He lifted her to his mouth and, with an evil grin, bent his head.

The first flutter of his tongue was light, soft. The touch a mere flicker of sensation but still her hips lifted seeking more.

He flattened his palms and smoothed his hands along her belly, pressing as he deepened the erotic kiss. The pressure built again, deep inside her the buzz of arousal increased. Maria gripped his forearms, needing to anchor herself to something. She was floating in a spiral of ecstasy. Her mind focused on the points where he touched her.

He licked at her clit, each flick and suck ramping her higher. Her body tightened, constricted, as she tried desperately to stay aware of everything, His hot palms scraped her ribcage and his fingers plucked at her nipples. The twin assaults pummeled her overloaded senses.

Her thighs splayed open, draped over his bunched muscles as he held her up for the intimate kiss. Her legs trembled as the sensations built in her body, overwhelming her, overtaking her thoughts until she could only feel—the wet suction of his mouth, the rough calluses of his fingers against her nipples, the gentle scrape of his teeth over her clit, and the tight grip of his arms. She knew that when she flew apart, he would catch her and keep her safe.

Pressure built, filling her like helium in a balloon, and her body became lighter until she burst in an explosion of light and sound and sensation. She arched her sex against his mouth, incoherent as her orgasm broke over her in waves of pleasure. Her belly clenched rhythmically, searching for him, as her sex wept. White lights flashed in her eyes, like fireworks rendering her blind and deaf to everything but the drumbeat of her heart.

Her loud moans penetrated in the small room.

"I need you," she gasped. The pulses low in her belly went on and on. Her entire body buzzed in the aftermath, like a live wire searching for an outlet, her consciousness flitted from moment to moment, needing more. Needing Dwayne.

The gentle laps of his tongue eased her down from the intense sensory explosion. But it still wasn't enough.

He soothed and petted her until her heartbeat slowed and her mind returned to awareness. With a gentle kiss against her soft inner thigh, Dwayne lifted from her body. She lay sprawled across the quilt too wrecked to move.

Her gaze tracked his movements, and suddenly she was aware of the giant bulge. He was huge.

"You must be hurting." Her voice was husky with her release.

"I'll be fine." Dwayne dropped onto his back and lay next to her, his arm thrown over his face, the muscles in his neck straining.

He wasn't fine.

Maria rolled to her side and propped her head on one hand, resting on her elbow.

She wanted to explore him. "So far you're the only one who got to play."

He groaned out a laugh.

Maria traced the happy trail of his minimal chest hair down the center of his body. The heat radiating off him was insane. She circled his belly button, and his stomach contracted away from her touch. As if he was so sensitive he couldn't even stand the brush of her fingers.

She reached the button at his jeans but his erection was so big the denim barely held him in, the fabric so tight it must be painful. "Let me ease that for you."

She cupped him through the thick rough weave. Heat seared her fingers.

He growled. "Not a good idea."

"I think it's a great idea." She explored the long hard length, wanting desperately to touch him. To do all the things to him that she'd read about just this afternoon.

"Maria—"

She worked at the button of his fly. "Dwayne. Let *me* play."

His hips rose as she stroked him through the material. "Think how much better this would be if you were naked," she said boldly.

She finally got his button open and lowered the zipper on his jeans carefully. Dwayne had his arm over his eyes and he held incredibly still as if he was holding back. Holding himself in check. She tried to ease his jeans off but his erection was so big that she was afraid she'd hurt him.

"I want these damn things off," she begged, "Help me."

"Your wish is my command." Dwayne lifted his hips and pushed his jeans down his thighs. But she wanted them all the way off. She tugged the material until it was around his knees and from there Dwayne finished the job.

Maria pushed his briefs down until his cock sprang free. "You're big."

"I'm a big guy." But he laughed.

Her fingers curled around the thick stalk and squeezed. She brushed her thumb over the head. Hot and smooth. A drop of pearly liquid coated the tip. "I didn't expect it to be so…."

"Impressive?"

She shot a look at him, but his eyes were sparkling with mirth. He clearly didn't have any insecurity issues about his size. "Bendy."

He muffled the shout of laughter.

But while he was laughing, she bent her head and licked that drop of semen from the tip.

Dwayne stopped laughing. "You don't need—"

Maria flushed. "Want," she murmured around the bulbous head. Then she wrapped her lips around him and fluttered her tongue against the head.

He flopped to the mattress. "You're sure?"

"Do you typically protest this much when a woman wants to suck your cock?"

Dwayne sputtered. "What the hell, Maria?"

"Just wondering if I'm special." The words were garbled because she talked while she explored him with her mouth.

"You are special," he said fiercely. "And don't you forget it."

HE WAS GOING TO HELL.

Right after she took him to heaven.

She bent her head again.

This was supposed to be about Maria, not about him. He hadn't planned for a blow job.

He wouldn't stop her, couldn't stop her. Because he wasn't about to tell her that her instincts were wrong.

She closed her mouth over the head of his erection and sucked.

She tongued him, then swallowed him whole, penetrating her throat the way he wished he could penetrate her body. But he'd promised and he refused to go back on his word. He'd keep that promise even if it meant blue balls for a month. Because she *was* special.

Her silky hair brushed his belly. She braced one soft hand on his thigh, while the other played with his balls as if she'd done this a thousand times.

Had she practiced on someone else?

Rage bubbled up in a geyser of jealousy, surprising the hell out of him. He had no say regarding who she did this with.

She took a long draw and his eyes rolled back in his head. "You're going to be the death of me."

Maria moaned around his erection.

The simple vibration shimmied through him. Fuck, he got even harder.

Suck. Lick.

She knelt on the homey quilt as if bowing in

supplication to his cock. Her eyes were closed and the look of sheer bliss on her face caused something to shift inside him. A seismic event of epic proportions.

He'd prided himself on being a generous lover, but he'd also expected to receive something too. Release. Satisfaction. Pleasure. But when he'd suggested this, he hadn't expected anything. Hadn't cared if he got off. But she did. And her enthusiasm was killing him.

He wanted to give her more. Give her so much pleasure she would drown in it.

She loved what she was doing, but he knew he could make this even better.

Dwayne curled up.

She let go of his erection with a pop. Her mouth glistened and her eyes were slumberous and for a second all he could do was stare at her. "You're so gorgeous." He brushed a strand of hair from her cheek.

She flushed but didn't speak.

"Do you trust me?"

She blinked. "Of course."

Her easy acceptance, no hesitation, humbled him.

"Hold on." He lifted her at the hips.

"You don't want me to keep going?" She trailed a single finger over his throbbing cock.

"Yes." He swung her body around and lay back down so that she was on all fours above him, her pussy right over his face.

"Oh." Maria ducked her head, her hair tumbled over his thighs, and he thought he might explode right then and there. She smiled at him through the tunnel between their bodies. "I've read about this. It sounded…interesting."

Dwayne lifted his head and lapped at her folds, taking

special care to purse his lips around her clit and suck. "I'm betting that it feels even better."

Her breath blew over his cock.

"I'm all for experimentation." She licked at his cockhead then sucked him into her mouth.

Dwayne cupped her stunning ass in his hands and pressed her pussy down onto his face.

"Excellent," he murmured. "I'm happy to be your subject."

MARIA COLLAPSED on the bed in a puddle of satisfaction.

So many firsts and she'd gotten to experience them with Dwayne, her crush, her fantasy.

"Thank you." She smiled softly.

"Don't thank me." His head lolled to the side. "The pleasure was all mine. And yours hopefully."

She wanted to giggle. Again. What was it about him that pulled forth the laughing happy girl that she'd been before?

Their playing had progressed beyond what she'd expected. She'd managed to convince him to cast aside his worries. "Any regrets?"

He shook his head, but he was staring above the dresser at the framed photograph of the lake as if his thoughts were far away.

He had curled his arm around her shoulder and pulled her close. Maria shivered and he tugged the old-fashioned quilt over their naked bodies. But he kept her snug against his side, her head resting on his shoulder.

"Not anymore."

"You have old ones?"

"After my dad…died, my whole life changed." He'd told her. He'd quit football and gone home to help his mother.

"His death fundamentally changed me. Up until that point I'd been focused. My plan was to go to college, get a degree, then the NFL, then take care of my family. I had my future mapped out, figuring I could live in the moment when I was older. But after 9/11, I realized that life was fragile."

Maria tried to soothe him, smoothing her hand over his chest.

"Seize the moment," he whispered.

"Your new motto?"

"Grab hold of every day, every opportunity because who knows what tomorrow will bring."

"That's so…courageous."

He shrugged, shifting her head into the curve of his neck. Without thinking, she licked a path to his jaw.

"Where do you find the courage to put what you want out there?"

"Me?" Maria blinked. "I don't have courage."

"Sweetheart, you're the epitome of bravery."

"Not anymore." Maria traced lazy circles around his nipple, watching the tiny bud rise. "Sometimes I think I used it all up when I escaped."

He lifted her hand to his mouth and kissed each fingertip reverently. "You're a miracle. And you have more courage than anyone I've ever known."

"When I was fifteen and trapped, all I wanted was for Prince Charming to swoop in and rescue me." She hid her face in his neck. "Isn't that dumb?"

"You don't need a prince."

She couldn't help but think that now he was talking about himself, not some fictional prince in a fairy tale.

But she knew the truth. Princes didn't exist, and the only person you could count on was you.

"You rescued yourself."

"Isn't that always the way?" she said wryly. She didn't want to waste this time talking about this. She nipped the tight skin of his jaw, telling him silently to move on. "Whatever. That's in the past."

Dwayne skimmed his fingers over her collarbones and down to toy with her nipple. "I'm more interested in the present."

"Me too." She arched under the erotic caress.

And they seized the moment, reaching again for mutual pleasure.

Chapter Thirteen

Maria woke to an empty bed.

Not a surprise. She'd have been shocked if Dwayne had stayed. She had no expectations for the future.

If there was a pang around her heart…she'd get over it. Didn't she always?

She rose from the bed, deliciously sore between her thighs. So that's what sex was all about.

She had loved it.

She would have been thrilled if they'd kept going. But Dwayne was a man of his word. A protector. And they had only "played."

The odds of convincing Dwayne for another night, and actual sex, were nonexistent.

Her stomach growled. Loudly. All that exercise had given her an appetite.

She stretched unashamed and unselfconscious about her nudity. Her stomach rumbled again. She dug through the dresser drawer looking for something to wear upstairs to change. A pair of sky blue sweatpants and a big oversized sweatshirt were in the top drawer. Hopefully the Stones wouldn't mind if she borrowed their clothes. She could throw them in the wash later. She twisted her hair into a loose bun, held together with a pencil from the cup on the small dresser.

After sloppily pulling the covers over the bed—she'd wash the sheets later too—she fetched her mother's rosary from the nightstand and slid the old beads into the pocket on the front of the sweatshirt. She left her clothes on the bed, figuring she'd wash them too.

She rubbed the beads and thought about how she would give anything to see her mother again. Her mama would not have approved what she and Dwayne had done.

But times had changed. Maria had changed.

She headed toward the stairs. When she walked through the kitchen, Dwayne was there.

"Oh, uh, good morning."

"Morning." He was stiff, awkward.

Really? He was going to play it this way?

"How are you feeling?" His gaze lingered on her sensitive breasts under the soft cotton fleece sweatshirt and then dropped to the V of her legs where her sex was tender.

"Fine."

She was. Disappointed about his reaction but otherwise fine.

She refused to retreat so she gave up her plan to go upstairs. To combat the awkwardness, she needed something to do with her hands so she started breakfast.

She pulled the ingredients for making omelets from the refrigerator. Precisely she laid the eggs, milk, cheese, peppers, onions, and broccoli in a row.

Dwayne watched silently as she retrieved the salt, pepper, and paprika from the spice shelf.

"Why do you do that?" He gestured to the row of ingredients.

Conversation. Stilted, and yet he wasn't running away in horror. If anything she thought she would be the awkward one. But there was no shame in what they'd done. Dwayne waited expectantly.

"It's called *mise en place*."

"What's that mean?"

"Everything in place before you begin."

With efficient movements, she began to chop the onions with a large chef's knife. "When I had reception, which wasn't always, I got three channels on my television. The Public Broadcasting channel had reruns of *Jacques Pépin* and so I learned to cook." She laughed, the joy bubbling up. "I'm so thankful that I have access to food to make all the dishes I drooled over for years."

She clutched the whisk to her chest and stared out the window, zooming back to that small ugly room where she'd listen to Jacques Pépin in his French accent talk about cooking things she'd never heard of while she scraped at that cement.

"You are amazing."

"Oh, no." She shook her head and some hair fell from the makeshift bun. Before she could move, he gently tucked the strands behind her ear.

The contact buzzed through her, the tender gesture an anomaly with his big hands and hard muscled body. "Yes. Amazing."

In the hushed morning air, birds twittered outside the kitchen window, the refrigerator hummed, and the heat whooshed as the furnace kicked on. But those sounds faded into the background as he stared into her eyes.

"You are a warrior. With the heart of an angel," he whispered.

She was no angel. She still clutched the whisk against her chest as he carefully removed the utensil from her fingers. "What are you doing?"

Stupid question.

Except she didn't know. She'd figured last night was going to be a singular experience. After all that was what he was known for. One-night stands.

Even though technically they hadn't had sex, she was pretty sure that he didn't go back for seconds, no matter what exactly transpired. And while yes, that was disappointing because holy wow would she like to do that again, today she was just thankful that he'd agreed to one time.

He cupped her face in his big palms, his thumbs rubbing against the curve of her cheeks, as he bent his head toward her.

"Seizing the moment." His breath coasted over her lips and then he was there. Firm, sensual, and a total surprise.

Maria melted into the kiss, her body awakening with a rush of arousal.

"Whoops!" Bitsy yelped.

Oh my God!

Maria tried to jump back, but Dwayne held firm, brushing her lips once before bussing her forehead.

"Glad someone is having fun," Bitsy muttered.

"WHAT CAN WE DO FOR YOU?" Dwayne stepped away from Maria, wishing he'd had more time alone with her. Although there wasn't anything else to say.

Last night was great but there wasn't going to be a repeat.

He introduced her to the pleasures of foreplay, of playing in general, but he wasn't sure she was ready for sex yet. The thought of her having sex with someone else made him want to punch something, or someone, but he'd get over it.

She wasn't his responsibility.

She *wasn't*.

He didn't know how many times he'd need to remind himself of that fact but he'd do it until he believed it.

"That's what is for breakfast?" Bitsy's horror at the healthy ingredients laid out on the counter pissed him off.

It was against company policy to murder the client but her constant bitching was going to send him over the edge.

"*You* can always cook for *us*."

Maria stifled a snicker.

"I don't know how to cook," Bitsy complained.

Maria turned away but not before he caught her smile.

"What do you usually make for breakfast?"

"I go downstairs and breakfast is on the buffet."

Jesus, could this girl be more privileged? Dwayne hesitated. He could use this to his advantage. "Well, if you're serious about disappearing, you're going to have to learn to cook. Why not learn now? I'm sure Maria won't mind."

He hated to throw Maria under the bus, but he wanted to press his advantage.

"Um. Okay sure."

Bitsy had come downstairs dressed up, from the tip of her ankle boots to her skinny jeans and silky top. She would be right at home in the audience at New York Fashion Week —and maybe he needed to stop picking up La'ei's *Vogue* since he knew that. Bitsy's hair was stick straight and shiny, her makeup heavy but perfect. Most men would be bowled over by her stunning looks, but her somewhat abrasive personality left him cold.

Maria, in her oversized sweats and tousled hair, her lips swollen from their kisses, and a tiny smudge of mascara at the corner of her eye, was rumpled and sexy. Bitsy wasn't in the same stratosphere of desirability.

Dwayne eased onto a stool at the counter and watched Maria patiently explained how to chop onions. Dwayne watched the girl struggle. Bitsy's attempt was clumsy, uneven and when she finished, her shoulders slumped.

"Not bad," Maria said.

Bitsy shrugged. "They aren't even like yours."

Maria frowned, a puzzled crinkle of her brows. "They don't need to be perfect to taste good. And it's your first try."

"Who taught you?"

Maria said, "I watch a lot of television and I practice a lot. I cook for myself most days. After time, I've gotten better. But honestly, I'm so grateful to have healthy food and the opportunity to cook that I don't care if the food comes out perfect."

Bitsy seemed to expect to get it perfect right away. What kind of upbringing made her so hard on herself?

Jill had said that the stepfather was difficult and dismissive. Maybe he should have paid attention rather than buying in to Bitsy as the stereotypical entitled rich bitch.

Bitsy rolled her eyes. "I'm done now."

Her tone was arrogant, but beneath the haughty attitude was an odd disgust. Dwayne couldn't figure her out.

Bitsy threw herself into the chair beside the massive floor-to-ceiling fireplace. The tower of river rock, strong and hearty, contrasted sharply with her dejected body language.

The fire warmed the great room, the sparks popping and the logs crackling cheerily.

Maria hummed as she assembled the omelets.

Dwayne sprawled out on the sofa, his long legs extended underneath the coffee table as he stared into the flames.

The entire scene radiated bucolic peace.

Bitsy's phone rang.

Everyone jumped.

ALIAS had replaced her old cell with an encrypted phone with the same number. But Kita controlled everything else.

"It's my mother." Bitsy sighed. "She's called four times since yesterday. I need to talk to her."

Technically she shouldn't talk to anyone, but they'd planned for this.

"Our encryption is impenetrable. Even if she is being monitored, they won't be able to figure out where you are. Go ahead and answer."

"Hello, mother."

So formal. So stiff. So annoyed.

"I'm at the spa. About to go in for a facial." Bitsy closed her eyes. "Yes, I know it will help with my skin issues."

Skin issues? Dwayne couldn't see a damn thing wrong with her skin.

Bitsy listened, then spoke. "Did you buy that new dress? It was really flattering, I'm sure Niles will love it."

Bitsy chatted with her mother about…nothing. "You should try out that new face cream I recommended in my column. It's supposed to be killer on wrinkles around the eyes. You'll look ten years younger for the fundraiser this weekend."

After a more platitudes and comments about clothing and makeup, Bitsy hung up. She threw her body back against the chair, eyes closed, phone still clutched in her hand.

Dwayne thought about when Bitsy had come into the office. "Did your mother know about the girlfriend?"

"They have an arrangement." Bitsy didn't even open her eyes.

Dwayne raised his brows.

"She looks good at his side for charity functions and fundraising events, and she ignores his little extras."

"More than one?" That could be another reason that Niles Vandenbeek had his mistress killed.

"Not at a time." Bitsy rolled her head back and forth.

"Why stay married?" Dwayne's concept of marriage had been shaped by his parents' loving relationship. He understood that people cheated, but why? He couldn't wrap his head around the reasons.

"She provides him with American citizenship and society connections."

Dwayne perked up. "What?"

"He's Swiss." Bitsy shrugged. "Besides how else would she support herself?"

Swiss. The same as the company that supplied the super expensive compounds for the drugs. "Is he involved with VDBC?"

"Oh, sure," Bitsy said. "That's his."

His company? Because if the Swiss company that supplied the base component was owned by Vandenbeek then he was gouging his own publicly held company in order to line his own pockets. "Are you sure?"

"Uh, yeah." Bitsy rolled her eyes. "I may not be the

brightest bulb in the bunch, but I know where the money comes from."

"You are smart."

"Whatever." Bitsy studied her nails. "Always know your source of support. Mother's words to live by."

Dwayne skimmed through his memory banks for information on the financials. "I noticed that rents on the DC properties are also high."

"He owns the house in DC and rents it back to Van Pharmaceuticals so he has a place to live when he's in the country."

"When?"

"Yeah, he splits his time between Geneva and the US." Bitsy twirled a strand of hair around her finger.

"Can I ask you some questions?"

"Why?"

"I gather information, whatever I can, about a situation. You never know when a stray piece of info will slot into place and connect all the dots."

"I guess. I don't really know if I can help though."

She'd already given him some unexpected intelligence.

"What else do you know about the way his businesses are intertwined?"

Dwayne pulled out his laptop and began making notes, asking questions about Niles Vandenbeek's business practices. "You realize some of these practices are unethical."

She rolled her head to look at him. "Wouldn't surprise me."

"So has the cost of the component for the asthma medicine really increased?"

She snorted. "No. He was bragging about it at dinner to my mother and me. The cost has actually decreased." She held out her hand, flashed a huge diamond. "That's why I got this ring."

Through this entire process Maria had been silent.

Now more than ever, he needed to convince Bitsy to go back to DC and testify at the Grand Jury inquisition about the inflated drug prices and tell the FBI about her stepfather's arrangement for the murder of his lover the lobbyist. But a pang of remorse nipped at him. Maria was counting on the proceeds of Bitsy's relocation fee to help her friends.

He couldn't afford to worry about her feelings. This guy needed to go down.

Bitsy rubbed at the screen on her phone, her face pensive.

"What's wrong?"

"I'm worried about my mother." Bitsy's gaze was uncertain. "I'm not sure how she will get along without me if I disappear. Who will look out for her?"

Her conversation with her mother had lasted about ten minutes. Based on her tone when she answered her phone and her general air of privilege, he hadn't anticipated her affection toward her mother. But Bitsy's body language told the story of annoyance and anxiety.

Bitsy sighed and tossed the brand new iPhone on the coffee table. "What if Niles hurts her?" She sat up, propped her elbows on her knees and her chin on her fisted hands.

Something was going on here. He'd told Jill that he had a bad feeling about Bitsy, but his boss had insisted on moving forward with this temporary protection.

"What happened that required Jillian to move up the timetable to get you out here?"

"I may have been snooping around my stepfather's home office."

"Does he keep anything there?"

"His most private files are at the house. He doesn't trust computers. He's got a separate home server just for those documents, and it isn't connected to the internet."

Dwayne tapped the file against his mouth. "If we could get into those files…."

"I know. But he came back early and caught me in his office. He was not happy with me. The only time we're allowed in there is when he's getting our jewelry out of his safe."

"Did he suspect you?"

She snorted. "I acted dumb and pretended to be trying to get this ring."

"Smart move." Dwayne rubbed his head. "Were you able to get anything?"

She lifted her phone and showed him her latest Instagram post. "My alter persona in New York is having way more fun than me," she said petulantly.

The Met in the background was perfect misdirection. Kita was a genius.

"This isn't about fun," he ground out, trying to figure out how he could make her change her mind and go back to give a deposition against her stepfather. "This is about a perversion of justice."

"Yada, yada, yada," Bitsy said. "This is me. Pretty and connected. Not—" she sniffed her fingers, which likely smelled like onions "—ugly and domesticated. My life is all about appearances."

"Aren't you upset about what your stepfather is doing?"

"I'm more concerned that when he finds out I overheard him, he'll kill me," she said flatly. She pressed her shoulders back and did a quick check of her clothes and makeup. As if preparing for a press conference. "He's already suspicious since he found me in his office."

"If you testify against him there's nothing he can do to you. He can't afford to harm you after it's done and you'll be safe."

She shuddered. "He can cut me off."

He was going about this all wrong. He needed to figure out how to turn her. How to convince her what was in it for her.

So far her mother seemed to be the only person she cared about. "If he's convicted your mother will be safe." Vandenbeek might only be fined for manipulating the price of the asthma drugs but he would go to jail for conspiracy to commit murder.

"And what do we do then?" Bitsy argued.

"Go on with your life."

"And how do I pay for that life?" She laughed harshly and gestured to her body. "This takes a lot of upkeep. This is all I know."

"You have a job." She wrote for the *Washington Post*. In the Style section.

"My job keeps me in shoes. That's it," she scoffed.

Dwayne could not put his finger on what bugged him about this girl but he had the urge to squeeze until she snapped and told him what her endgame was.

She clearly didn't want to give up the lifestyle her stepfather paid for. But then why come to ALIAS in the first place? If she disappeared how was she going to pay for her life?

Shit. This girl was getting to him.

Maria set up dishes on the island. Normally Dwayne would help but he needed to keep working on Bitsy. Maria shot a glare his way.

Was she paying attention to their conversation? How much had she overheard?

Jill's caution echoed in his mind. *Keep Maria out of this. She doesn't need the crisis of conscience. The parallels between her situation and Bitsy's are strong. I don't want her upset.*

But Bitsy's information had the potential to take down the drug company's unethical practices. Thousands would be unable to afford the life-saving drug if she didn't agree to give testimony on her stepfather and his illegal activities.

Vandenbeek had gerrymandered the system so that the Van Pharmaceuticals and VDBC would profit while putting kids at risk.

Getting her to rat on her stepfather was the right thing to do, but his stomach twisted at the notion that he was going to be hurting Maria. She wanted Bitsy's client fee to help her friends. He needed to figure out Bitsy's trigger point.

"How old are you?" he asked.

"Twenty-four."

Maria jolted.

"Same as her." Bitsy hadn't used Maria's name once.

"*Her* has a name."

"Well, let's face it, my situation is completely different from *Maria's.* She had nothing to lose while I've got everything to lose."

And that's what this was about. What she has to lose. But running away wouldn't help her. So what the hell was her plan?

And why did he feel that for all her posturing, he was missing something important?

Maria said, "Breakfast."

His chance to press the advantage was lost.

Chapter Fourteen

They ate breakfast in silence.

Maria had been listening carefully to Dwayne and Bitsy's conversation. She understood what he was trying to do, and the realization was a blow.

He was looking for a way to convince Bitsy to go back to DC and tell the authorities about her stepfather and his business dealings. His intent had been clear as day.

Dwayne knew she didn't want Bitsy to go back. Knew she wanted to help her friends, and if Adams-Larsen relocated Bitsy, part of the firm's fee would go to help Sophia and Graciela.

Her emotions were all over the map. But clearly she meant less than nothing to him if he was eagerly trying to get their potential client to give up the idea of a relo.

Bitsy glanced between them as if she could sense the tension. "I'm going to take a nap." She scuttled up the stairs, leaving her dishes on the table.

"You're quiet." He'd frowned at her during the meal. But mostly he'd studied Bitsy. Trying to figure out how to turn her, Maria guessed. She might have read Dwayne's personnel file, by accident. Or on purpose. He was an expert in getting witnesses to reveal their information.

Maybe he'd played her. Maybe all that talk of regrets and seizing the moment was to manipulate her into sexy times. Maybe he didn't give a shit about anyone. That wasn't how he came across but maybe she'd been wrong about him.

"You're trying to get her to be a witness." She tried to keep the hurt out of her voice.

"I...."

"Don't." She held up her hand. "Don't lie to me."

"Fuck it." Dwayne admitted, "Jill wants her to give testimony to a Grand Jury."

So he didn't trust Maria. "You could have told me."

"I didn't want to upset you."

She snorted and fought the urge to roll her eyes. But if Jill wanted Bitsy to testify against her stepfather, then Maria would do what she could to help.

"Bitsy needs to feel like she's in control."

"Why do you think that?" Dwayne asked.

"Everyone is making decisions for her. Her lack of agency isn't going to sway her to your cause." Maria had experience that couldn't be learned from a book. And she weirdly understood Bitsy.

"Okay." But he didn't sound like he believed it.

"I know I don't have a college degree," she said defensively. She'd recently passed her high school equivalency. "But I get her."

"School of life gives you insight that I don't have." Dwayne said, "I appreciate your input."

He opened his mouth, but she was done. Now she wanted to get personal. He'd ignored what she wanted regarding Bitsy without talking to her about it. So why would he refuse to have sex with her?

"What was last night's refusal really about?" she asked.

He hesitated. "Protecting you."

"I'm not a victim anymore." She had moved on. Why couldn't everyone see that?

"I never said you were." He sipped his coffee, his fingers loosely curled around the mug's handle. That's when she knew he was lying. He was a charge-straight-ahead guy who went full out on everything he did. His loose clasp meant he was trying too hard to stay relaxed.

She hadn't misread him. But how far would he go to pretend he was telling the truth?

"Then what're you protecting me from?"

"From me."

She laughed harshly. Oh no. He wasn't going to shove this off on her. She'd force him to be honest. "Bullshit. You're protecting yourself."

"What?"

"You're afraid to care for anyone. Afraid they'll leave. Afraid of adding anyone else to the careful circle of your family."

A coward.

Dwayne puffed his chest, bulking up, expanding as if he could physically take over the space and push away her impressions. But it wasn't going to work.

He narrowed his gaze. "You don't know anything about me."

"Ha." He could deny what he wanted but she'd learned a few things from Dr. Abboud.

The garage door rumbled, interrupting the tense standoff.

Dwayne jumped to his feet and put his body between

Maria and the intruders. His weapon, wherever it had come from, was locked and loaded.

Within seconds, she heard Bliss's voice. "Hey guys! It's Jack and Bliss."

Dwayne was saved by her old friends.

BLISS AND JACK STONE entered the kitchen of their cabin.

Jack Stone was a former Navy SEAL badass, with a massive chest, almost as large as Dwayne's, and harsh features, underscored by a scar bisecting one of his eyebrows. But he clearly loved his wife.

Bliss Lee Stone was a stunning mix of half Chinese and half Irish descent with rich auburn hair and a subtle sexuality. When Dwayne had worked with Bliss, she had always carried a slight air of melancholy. She'd been excellent at her job, and the ALIAS office definitely missed her, but California, and Jack, were clearly doing her right.

She glowed.

Bliss's genuine smile didn't dim, but when Dwayne leaned in for a hug she shot him a frown. "We're going to have a talk," she whispered.

"Sure."

Jack had Maria wrapped up in a tight hug. Dwayne didn't know Jack Stone well, but he didn't seem like the hugging type. Dwayne's tension rose as the hug went on longer than Dwayne liked.

"How are you?" Jack held on to Maria's shoulders and surveyed her from head to toe. His eyes narrowed, and then he shot Dwayne a look of censure.

What the actual hell?

Dwayne had a clear view down the hallway and the door to the guest room was partially open. Maria was wearing sweats with Lake Tahoe emblazoned down the side of the leg and across her chest. She hadn't been shopping since they got here, so she must have borrowed them from the guest room.

The guest room with the rumpled bed. Shit.

Dwayne smiled grimly. Because he knew how he'd feel if he thought some dick was taking advantage of Maria.

"What are you guys doing here?" Maria had a soft smile on her face.

"We came up to make sure the house was ready for you." Lie. Something else was going on.

Bitsy had descended at the commotion and sauntered into the kitchen.

"This is our friend, Bitsy." Maria introduced Bitsy politely as if they were up here for vacation instead of protection.

Bitsy eyed them speculatively. "This is your house?"

"Family cabin."

Cabin. Their idea of a cabin and Dwayne's were slightly different, but still he was happy for Bliss. Within six months, the Adams-Larsen office had lost two of their company family to the West Coast and the Stone brothers.

"How's Rissa?" Maria asked. "And John?"

Bliss smiled. "They're great. The new office is coming along."

Even Jack Stone looked more relaxed than Dwayne had ever seen him. Jack stretched, yawned. "I need a walk after that drive. Dwayne, you interested?"

While the request was clumsy, Dwayne had already

figured out that this was not a random question. "I could use the exercise."

"We'll just stay here and have some girl talk." Bliss grinned.

Maria's eyes widened and she looked like she wanted to escape.

"I assume I can't go for a walk with you." Bitsy glanced between them and the disdain on her face raised Dwayne's ire again. "I'm going back upstairs."

She stomped up the stairs like a kid throwing a tantrum.

As soon as Bitsy exited, Bliss demanded, "What is going on here?"

Bliss and Jack circled Maria, keeping Dwayne away from her as if they thought they knew her better than him. Jealousy. A sharp double-edged knife slid between his ribs and into his heart. "Excuse me?"

Maria put her hand on Bliss's forearm. "It's all good."

Jack confronted Dwayne. "You want to explain?" His voice was hard, uncompromising.

It wasn't like they were teenagers. Dwayne was annoyed, but he was also happy they cared. "We've got problems with Miss Heiress."

"We know. Kita called us." Bliss narrowed her gaze. "However, nothing is more important than Maria."

Dwayne had had enough. "Maria can take care of herself."

"She's vulnerable," Bliss shot back.

"She can handle anything." His testiness was evident in the sharp bite of his words.

Maria attempted to look indignant, but with the oversized sweats she couldn't quite pull it off. "*She* is right here."

Bliss said to Dwayne, still partially shielding Maria. "What's wrong with you?"

There was nothing wrong with him. He hadn't hurt her. Last night had been consensual. And none of their business.

"You don't need to coddle Maria." His instinct to get between them and Maria was wrong too. She was fully capable of sticking up for herself. She did it with him all the time. Even so, he wanted to be the one protecting her. That was crazy. The need jittered inside him like an angry swarm of bees buzzing, the feeling spread with every moment they blocked her from him.

Not to mention that she probably wanted nothing to do with him. She was pissed that he'd kept his objectives from her.

Jack bulked up. "What are your intentions?" The dude was big, but Dwayne could take him. Of course he'd be out of a job after assaulting the senior principle of the Stone Consulting and ALIAS partnership.

"Jesus, Jack." Maria pushed between them. "Leave Dwayne alone."

"He took advantage."

"*I* took advantage of *him*." Maria's voice rose. "You know his reputation. He was perfect."

And just that easily, she gutted him.

He hadn't intended to start anything permanent, but the reality that she'd used him made it difficult for him to catch his breath.

Shit.

How was that for irony? He'd spent months having one-night stands so that he wouldn't be tempted when all along that was all she wanted from him.

"You should have let me know that was your objective

sooner, sweetheart," he drawled. He couldn't seem to draw a complete breath, as if her admission were a snake wrapping around his lungs and squeezing the life from him. "I'll take that walk now."

Dwayne shoved out the back door and onto the deck. He breathed in the clean, crisp cold air and let the hurt wash over him. Then he took off down the path to the beach.

———

MARIA STARED AFTER DWAYNE. She'd hurt him.

Unbelievable.

She took a step toward the door.

"I'll just, uh…." Jack skated his big palm down Bliss's arm and squeezed her fingers, then beelined for the French doors.

That simple unconscious affection pierced her heart. Because that's what she wanted with Dwayne. Not just one night of passion but a connection that transcended words.

Bliss said, "Um, what just happened?"

"I'm a grown woman, you know." Maria watched Dwayne jog toward the lake. "Old enough to make my own decisions and my own mistakes."

"So Dwayne was a mistake?"

"Not at all." He wasn't. No matter what happened going forward, Dwayne Lameko had given her an incredible night of pleasure. While she couldn't think of a better man to give her virginity to, that apparently wasn't going to happen. The look on his face when he'd left made her feel like she'd just lost something precious.

Maria shook off the melancholy and began cleaning up the kitchen.

"Sorry the kitchen is a mess. We just finished breakfast." She kept her head down as she scraped most of Bitsy's omelet down the disposal. She hated to waste the food, but she didn't know what else to do with it. "Oh, are you hungry?"

"Maria, you don't need to wait on us." Bliss grabbed a dishcloth and began cleaning.

"I know." Maria shook her head. "What you don't understand is I like cooking for people. It isn't about gratitude to you. It's about being thankful I have people to cook for."

She glanced out the window again, but Dwayne and Jack had disappeared.

"You really are okay?" Bliss asked.

"Of course I am." She'd survived a madman. She'd survived imprisonment. She'd survived escape. And she'd survived testifying against José Fernandez. She could handle anything.

But Bitsy Vandenbeek could not. It had barely been three days since she'd come to the ALIAS office and the girl was going stir crazy. Maria's instincts were humming. Bitsy seemed like she was ready to bolt. And as much as she hated to admit it, Dwayne had been correct. When they'd taken this case he'd objected, saying there was more going on here. Her heart gave a pang and she glanced longingly out the window. But wishing him back wasn't going to get things done.

"We've got a problem." Maria confessed.

Bliss ran her hand through her red hair. "More than one?"

"I don't know, but Bitsy isn't handling this mini-vacation well."

"She did seem quick to run upstairs."

Maria glanced out the back window again. Thought about the client fee that ALIAS wasn't going to receive. The despair at letting her friends down was immense, even if they didn't know that she'd been contributing when she could.

"What's wrong?"

Maria glanced around the multi-million dollar "cabin" as she wiped down the counter. She could ask Bliss for a donation for S.S.A.F.E. But the truth was, Bliss and Jack and the rest of the Stone family had given her more than she could ever repay. They'd protected her and helped her re-enter society. "She doesn't have the temperament to disappear."

"So what are we going to do about it?"

"I don't know."

"You know about her stepfather?" Bliss asked.

"Yes." Maria loaded the dishwasher. "He is putting profit and greed above the wellbeing of children who depend on his medicine."

"He's evil."

"I think so." So what Maria needed to do was convince the girl that she had to tell he authorities what she knew. She couldn't let him get away with what he'd done. There was no way Bitsy would handle changing her identity and relocating. Not to mention that Maria didn't want ALIAS to take her as a client. She didn't think Bitsy would adhere to the rules regarding ALIAS's security measures or keep their secrets.

Maria leaned against the sink and lifted her head to stare at the white ceiling. "She has no confidence."

"That girl?" Bliss laughed.

But Maria didn't. "He's degraded her self-worth. She

believes her only assets are looking good and being well-connected."

Maria couldn't fathom that. Of course, Maria had refused to accept the expectations and limitations people had tried to place on her in the name of protecting her. She had declared that she wasn't a victim. Not anymore. She had seized ownership of herself.

"Bitsy needs to learn to acknowledge and celebrate her strengths," Maria said. "But that isn't going to happen overnight." And they couldn't wait.

"You think she'll bolt?" Bliss asked.

"She's thinking about it."

"What do you suggest?" Bliss leaned against the countertop, waiting for Maria's input.

Her heart swelled. She could do this. Maria thought about Bitsy's wistfulness while looking at the spa pics. "We need to get her out for a few hours so she sees what she's going to be missing. Maybe something at the nearby hotel spa."

Maria kissed the fee goodbye.

"What if I get you massage appointments?" Bliss started the dishwasher.

"She'd probably like it. But I can't expense a massage." Maria entered the information for employee reimbursements. She was pretty sure an expensive massage wasn't on the approved list.

"I've got it." Bliss's eyes sparkled.

"Are you going to come with us?"

"No. I'll stay here and brainstorm with Dwayne and Jack about how to convince our errant client to return to DC and testify. You got this."

And it would give Maria time away from Dwayne. He'd probably be happy she was gone for a while.

"I don't want Bitsy knowing what we do," Maria said fiercely. She'd already shown that her main concern was selfish. Even as Maria had sympathy for Bitsy's plight, she needed to protect ALIAS. Right now, Bitsy suspected what they did, but she didn't know for sure. "She only cares about herself." And ALIAS couldn't afford to reveal their secrets.

Chapter Fifteen

"Ah, Civilization," Bitsy said with relief as she and Maria entered the spa after Bliss dropped them off.

"Are you seriously complaining about our accommodations?" Maria wanted to smack her. But she knew some of her frustration stemmed from the unsettled confrontation with Dwayne.

"It's not the house. It's the fact that we haven't been out in days."

Not even two days. Maria had spent almost three thousand days alone. "How did you ever think you were going to handle disappearing?"

An odd look crossed over Bitsy's face. Maria's intuition buzzed but they entered the hotel spa and she figured they could deal with whatever was going on when they got back to the cabin.

When they checked in, the hostess said, "Here's a special beverage just for you."

She smiled at them like she had a secret and handed them each a glass of champagne. Another woman led Bitsy and Maria to the locker room. "Change in here. Take off all your clothes. Leave your belongings in the locker and use the robe provided. No cell phones."

Maria nodded, smiled, and had no intention of leaving her cell in the locker. She never went anywhere without it.

Ever.

"Once you're ready, please make yourself comfortable in the waiting room."

She stripped self-consciously and hurriedly wrapped up in the thick cotton robe, tucking her cell in the pocket when Bitsy wasn't looking. She also added her rosary; needing the comfort, she threaded her fingers through the beads, worrying at them.

They walked down the hallway to the waiting room, where a credenza held a water dispenser, fruit slices floating in the refreshment, and a platter with various healthy treats. Bitsy squealed softly and loaded a plate with the small appetizers. While they waited, Maria sipped her champagne, so she didn't draw attention rather than because she wanted the alcohol.

Bitsy chugged her glass in one gulp.

They sat on the rattan furniture and waited for their names to be called. Bitsy was acting strange. She seemed nervous. Her hands fluttered like when she'd originally come into the ALIAS office.

"You okay?" Maria asked.

"I'm not like you," Bitsy said mournfully.

"What does that mean?"

"I read all about you, you know."

Okay, Maria had no idea where this was heading but she damn sure knew it was no place good.

She could care less but Bitsy seemed to think a response was necessary. "I'm flattered."

"You were a hero." Her bright emerald eyes had dimmed, her lids dipped, and she tilted her head in a wistful manner. "You took control."

"I had no choice." Maria couldn't believe this girl. She would still be stuck in that basement, or dead, if she hadn't rescued herself.

"I'm not that brave." Bitsy shook her head, her eyes sad, almost defeated. "Talking with you and Dwayne made me realize I don't have it in me."

What was going on here? Maria was getting a bad feeling about this. "It?"

"I was fooling myself. I can't disappear."

So she would testify against her stepfather? Dwayne would be happy. Maria didn't know how she felt. Niles Vandenbeek was a criminal and a bad man. He needed to be stopped. Regret simmered in her heart. She'd wanted to help Graciela and Sophia but not at the expense the thousands who would be harmed by his actions. It wasn't the right thing to do.

She knew that.

Acknowledged that and still….

"Speaking with the authorities is the right thing to do," Maria said gently.

Bitsy rubbed her palms down the front of her robe. "Yeah, it is. If you're strong enough, smart enough." Bitsy's melancholy tone had her on edge.

"No one starts out strong." Maria tried to tell her. "You have to try every day to take another step toward strength." Or another scratch of a plastic spoon against concrete. "And when you get discouraged just keep going."

"It's too late for me," Bitsy said.

Maria was beginning to wish that Bliss was at the spa with Bitsy. She didn't belong here. Didn't want to belong here. Maria worried at the rosary beads and reached for a calm she couldn't seem to find. She drank more champagne.

The room was stuffy and her eyelids drooped. She blinked hard, shook her head to clear it.

As if a veil had dropped over her face, the room fuzzed. The weird haziness increased.

Eventually they were the only two women left in the waiting room. A door behind a screen opened. "Elizabeth?"

The guy who called Bitsy's name was huge. As big as Dwayne. Maybe bigger.

Everyone else who'd opened that door had been a woman or a smaller man. This guy did not look like a massage therapist.

"I don't have a good feeling about this," she whispered to Bitsy.

But when she glanced at Bitsy, the woman was passed out cold.

"Let's go." He seemed impatient.

"I don't think my friend is feeling well." Maria tried to smile but her mouth wouldn't curve. "We'll pass."

The man frowned at her, strode forward. Something was wrong.

"Are you with her?" the brute asked.

She didn't want to answer but her head bobbed forward. Protect the client. Adams-Larsen and Jill were counting on her to protect Bitsy. "Yaasss."

The man reached for Bitsy.

"You can't take her." Maria tried to jump up, but her limbs didn't cooperate, her feet tangling as she tried to stand. She tipped forward and fell on the opposite cushioned sofa, her face bounced against the cushion. She couldn't lift her arms to break her fall.

The man grabbed her and slung her over his shoulder.

Maria tried to call out but her vocal cords didn't work properly.

Her hair mostly hid her face, but she could see another guy pick up Bitsy, who was definitely unconscious. "Thought it was one."

"They're together."

They opened a door that led outside instead of into the spa.

Maria opened her mouth to scream but a soft wheeze escaped.

Kita's self-defense training whooshed from her head as panic took over. *Not again. Not again.*

Maria's thoughts pinged around her brain like plastic lottery balls. Then her sanity returned. Hell no. Not again.

She kicked her feet against the guy's stomach. He grunted but besides that didn't make a sound. She twisted, trying desperately to break free but her coordination sucked and all it did was make him swear.

Bitsy wasn't struggling.

Drugged. They'd been drugged.

He slung Maria into the backseat of a large SUV. She lay limply across the seat.

Think, think.

The phone!

She clumsily reached in the robe pocket, but she couldn't get her fingers to work properly as she desperately tried to press the panic button on her phone.

The alert should go to everyone at ALIAS. They'd be able to track her by the GPS signal. She wasn't helpless. She'd never be helpless again. She just had to press that button and then hold on until they came to their rescue. She had to be smart. Protect the client.

But the harder she concentrated, the less her fingers

wanted to work. They slipped over the buttons, her brain unable to coordinate. A prick at her neck was her only warning. More drugs. Shit.

She seriously wasn't this unlucky.

DWAYNE AND JACK got back to the house drenched in sweat. They'd run out their aggression. Jack had initially glowered at him but after a mile or so, he'd backed off.

Maria's tacit dismissal, the fact that she used him, burned beneath his breastbone. She used him. All that worry about her feelings, about taking advantage of her, and she managed to throw one over on him. Nothing personal.

It was stupid to be upset. It wasn't as if he'd seen a future for them. Yet, the gnawing in his gut hadn't abated even after they'd upped their walk to a brisk run along the frigid lake.

Dwayne and Jack climbed the steps to the deck. He grabbed the sweatshirt he'd stripped off earlier and yanked it over his head. In his pocket, his cell began to buzz. Jack's too.

Dwayne frowned as Bliss burst out the back door.

"Oh my God." She was waving her phone.

Jack rushed his wife and wrapped his arms around her shaking body. "What's wrong?"

"Maria," Bliss gasped.

"Where is she?" But Dwayne was reading the information from the alert he'd missed while running on the shore.

His phone rang. It was Kita.

"What's going on?" he demanded.

"That's what I'd like to know," Kita said. "Maria is on the move. The plan was to sit on Bitsy at the house and not go anywhere."

He'd been an idiot. Because he'd been butt hurt, he'd left without confirming that they were going to stay put.

"It's complicated." Dwayne turned to Bliss. "Where did they go?"

Bliss was wringing her hands. "The spa. I dropped them off about thirty minutes ago."

"The spa," Dwayne said flatly.

"We were trying to show Bitsy what she'd be missing." Bliss wrapped her arms around her waist.

"Yeah, well, they were there about twenty minutes and then they started moving."

"Where are they now?" Dwayne tried to keep the panic out of his voice. Panic wouldn't help Maria.

"I was tracking her cell, but she's stopped moving." Kita hesitated.

Urgency pulsed through him. "She wouldn't leave the spa without informing us."

"Unless she was pissed," Bliss whispered.

"Was she?"

"I didn't think so." Bliss rested her forehead against Jack's neck and inhaled deeply. She turned to face him. "But let's face it, she has a history of bolting."

"Bullshit." Dwayne frowned at his former coworker. "She would never put the client in jeopardy and she would never do that to me." Rage bubbled up with an alarming force. "To ALIAS," he corrected. "Something is wrong."

"Maybe Bitsy took off and Maria went after her?" Bliss broke away from Jack.

That idea had merit.

"Bitsy was definitely getting cabin fever."

Dwayne wanted to latch on to that idea, but he still couldn't shake the conviction that Maria would not have let her leave. She knew what was at stake.

"Bliss, you stay here in case they come back. Dwayne and I will start searching." Jack directed.

"Check the spa and see if they have any idea where they went." Bliss grabbed Jack's arm. "Bring her home."

Dwayne was still on the phone with Kita. "Give me her last known location." She bulleted out the coordinates.

Jack jumped in his SUV and Dwayne took the Range Rover. "Keep me posted," he snarled at Jack.

Dwayne drove like a maniac until he got to the location Maria's GPS had stopped transmitting.

Except it was nothing. The spot was right at the intersection of 267 and Highway 28 at the King's Beach roundabout. The lake was to his left so he had three options, go back to Incline Village, go straight toward Tahoe City, or go right and head up the mountain toward Truckee. That road also led to Highway 80, and if they hit I80, his search would have to expand even farther.

"Fuck!" he shouted. His heart pounded so hard he thought it would bang right out of his chest. She could be anywhere. Jack's number popped up on his phone.

"Tell me you found them," Dwayne begged hoarsely.

"I'm sorry, they're both gone. No one saw anything. When the spa employees entered the waiting room, they weren't there. The hostess said that a guy dropped off a special bottle of champagne because he wanted to surprise his fiancée. I got the half empty bottle and we can try to get prints and test the alcohol for sedatives, but both of those things will take time we don't have."

"Shit. They were probably drugged." Dwayne thought

frantically. "But Maria doesn't drink. So maybe she'll be able to get away."

Except she wouldn't leave Bitsy. She took her responsibilities with ALIAS seriously. After his meltdown during the setup phase of this mission, she was just stubborn enough not to leave Bitsy to prove he was wrong about her ability to handle this job. He was desperate and grasping at straws. "What about security cameras at the spa?"

"Getting the recordings now." Jack suggested. "Let's buddy up. We need both eyes on this."

Fuck. What had he been thinking? He'd left the house in anger. Pissed and hurt. Never leave without saying goodbye. He knew that.

Dwayne took a deep breath. Let it out slowly.

"She's strong. And she's smart. And she can kick ass." He kept repeating those words like a mantra as he drove to meet Jack at the spa.

By the time Dwayne arrived, Jack had already looked at the tapes. Jack's expression gutted Dwayne. "No." As if he could stop this nightmare. As if by denying it he could just rewind and go back to the kitchen this morning.

"You sure you want to see this?"

"Is she—" *dead?*

"Struggling."

"Thank God."

"Bitsy was out," Jack said. "But the guy carrying Maria had a difficult time. She wasn't making it easy on him."

Pride filtered through his fear. *Good job, la'u manamea. I'm coming for you.*

"We need copies so we can run faces through the FBI's FACE program."

"Already on it." Jack clamped a hand on Dwayne's shoulder. "We're going to get them back."

Dwayne vacillated between knowing Maria could save herself—"She's got balls. She saved herself once"—and worrying. Because what if she didn't think anyone would come for her?

When he left the cabin, he'd been angry. She'd used him. And she'd let him know. What if she thought he'd hold that against her?

His phone rang. Kita. Dwayne answered as he and Jack headed back toward Maria's last known location. She conferenced Bliss in on the call.

"I don't understand how they found Bitsy." Dwayne took the passenger seat and let Jack drive. "Private jet. No passenger manifest. Kita rented the car. We followed a strict protocol so that she could disappear temporarily."

Jack was silent.

"It doesn't make any sense."

Kita said, "I'm working on what happened right now. Bitsy seems to have made at least one unauthorized call."

Bitsy did this? Dwayne clenched his fists so tightly his veins popped hard. "They could be anywhere." If Bitsy made a call, why had they taken Maria too?

Kita said, "I need to alert Jill that Maria and the client have been compromised."

"Compromised doesn't even cover it." Dwayne swore. "Shit, Kita."

"I know. Let me loop in Jill and then we'll figure out what to do next. I'll call you back in ten."

"Make it five."

Fear struck his heart. Maria had to be okay.

"She escaped before." Dwayne couldn't help but repeat.

"She did." But Jack sounded like he was humoring Dwayne. "But you have to be prepared. I saw her after she ran away the first time. She was scared and couldn't handle being around people."

"She can handle anything." But her fear that she'd used up all her courage niggled at his mind. Could being kidnapped again throw her over the edge?

No. Dammit. She was going to be fine. He refused to accept any other outcome.

Chapter Sixteen

A dank musty smell, the odor of dirt and decay, surrounded Maria.

Dear God, was she back in the cellar? No. *No.* The cellar had blown up in a giant fireball. She wasn't back there. She was here. Wait, where?

Her head pounded and her neck was sore. She slitted her eyes open, then blinked. Nothing looked familiar. Where…what? She squeezed her eyes shut and tried to remember. The giant man. Bitsy out cold.

Beside her, Bitsy groaned.

When Maria tried to push to sitting, her arms resisted. At first, she thought she was still suffering from whatever drug they'd given her.

But cold, hard metal was tight around her wrists. She'd been handcuffed! Slogging through the molasses of her brain, a thick viscous veil covered her memory. The last thing…her phone.

But when she shoved her cuffed hands into the robe's pocket, the phone was gone.

For a moment, despair overwhelmed her.

Kidnapped. Bound. Helpless.

But then rage burned away the fogginess and the hopelessness. She was not going to be a victim again.

She yanked hard, trying to pull her arms apart. The cuffs abraded her wrists and they began to throb.

Bitsy groaned. "Oh my God, my head hurts."

Maria pushed up against the wall. They were on a bare mattress on dirty beige carpeting. So she had a clear view of Bitsy's face when the girl figured out she was handcuffed.

Bitsy stared at her wrists with confusion, then shook her arms like she couldn't believe they had restrained her. "What is happening?"

"We've been kidnapped," Maria said calmly but inside she was screaming.

"How?" Bitsy blinked, her eyes still woozy.

"I think the champagne was drugged." Maria's brain was still not working at full speed. "But how would they know we were there?"

Bitsy's guilty face told her.

"What did you do?"

"I was just trying to make plans," she said defiantly.

"Plans!" Maria's voice rose as she realized that Bitsy had told someone she was in Tahoe. "What kind of plans?"

"I told my stepfather I would make a deal with him."

Maria wanted to bang her head against the wall. "Why would you do that? You were supposed to be staying *safe*. Adams-Larsen was protecting you."

"I had reasons." Bitsy averted her gaze, shifting her eyes up and to the right. "Besides, it was boring."

"You jeopardized our lives because you were bored?" Maria was so disgusted. Fear had been replaced by rage.

Something about the way Bitsy answered tugged at Maria's consciousness. Bitsy was lying.

"I don't want to go into hiding anymore." Bitsy's lips trembled. "I don't know what it would do to my mother. I just want my life back."

Maria's hands balled into fists. But right now, they needed to focus on escape—anything else was counterproductive.

"What did you think you were going to accomplish by calling him?" She made it sound like a command. She remembered Dwayne's words. Gather as much as information as possible to put together the full picture.

Bitsy tried to stand, but she fell to her knees with a cry, then tipped forward to catch herself on her hands. She held there on all fours breathing heavily. The girl's thin wrists extended from the wide sleeves of the spa robe. Her head hung down between her arms.

"Not this." When she lifted her head, tears shimmered in her eyes. "I might have screwed up."

Cold slithered through Maria, insidious. Bitsy had given away her location to the man who had his girlfriend killed solely because of greed. He'd have no compunction about killing them. "Tell me."

"The whole point was to get money from my stepfather."

"What whole point?" But Maria was afraid she knew. This girl had set herself up, for money?

"I wanted an assurance that if I kept quiet, he'd support me and my mother." Tears trailed down her cheeks.

"You told your stepfather what you overheard?"

"Yes," she whispered.

"What else?" Maria demanded, because she was pretty sure there was more.

"I may have stolen some evidence from his office."

That's why she had Jill move up the timetable on this mission. "So he would give you money?"

Bitsy bit her lip and nodded. "In exchange for my promise not to tell."

She'd been trying to blackmail a man who'd had his mistress killed for knowing the same information.

"It didn't occur to you that this could backfire?"

"I'm Bitsy Vandenbeek," she said imperiously.

"How's that working out for you?" Sarcasm laced her words.

"I'm not very bright. You know? My whole life my stepfather told me I needed to just look pretty." Bitsy shook her head. "I didn't want to believe he was right," she whispered. "I was trapped with no way to support myself or my mother."

Maria thought furiously. "You're smarter than that." But by calling her stepfather she'd fulfilled his prediction.

"He was supposed to give me his answer later today." Bitsy looked around the bare room. "I didn't expect him to do this. And I certainly didn't expect him to find me this fast."

Maria hadn't survived one kidnapping to die in another. "No way are we waiting around for them to kill us."

The light in the room was dim. The windows were shuttered from the outside. Maria stood shakily and made her way to the single window. She tugged on the sash, but it was locked. Apparently from the outside.

She peered in the small closet. A lone wire hanger swung on the pole.

The room had a single mattress with no sheets and one lamp, no shade.

They couldn't dig their way out. While starting a fire

might get someone's attention, because the window was locked, she'd be signing their death sentence.

Think.

The cold seeped through the thin carpeting and froze her bare feet. Maria shivered.

"We need to come up with a plan."

Bitsy crouched in a ball in the corner. "But I don't want to be hurt. I want to get my life back."

Unbelievable.

Maria considered their options. If the stepfather had wanted them dead, he would have already had them killed. But it would look awfully strange if his mistress and his stepdaughter both died under mysterious circumstances.

Maria tried again to break the cuffs. The wire hanger. She grabbed it but the end was too thick to try and jimmy the hard metal restraints.

Maria roamed the room, searching for anything to help them get the hell out of here. "We need to get out."

"How are we going to do that?"

She clutched at the pocket of her robe and the hard beads of her mother's rosary curled around her fingers.

Immediately the prayer beads soothed her.

She wasn't alone anymore. She had friends who would be looking for her. She just needed to do everything she could to escape and rescue Bitsy.

She thought about Dwayne. He wouldn't leave her here. He *wouldn't.*

But she couldn't sit around and hope that she'd be rescued.

They were going to have to outsmart their captors. And to do that, Maria needed Bitsy's help. There was no way she could overpower two guards alone, assuming they were both still here.

But before she did, she was getting this bitch to agree to inform on her stepfather.

"I'm going to get us out of here." Maria wasn't about to die now.

"How?" Bitsy appeared despondent.

"You have to agree to give a deposition about what your stepfather did."

"But—"

"Don't you understand? This isn't about you. Or me. It's about doing what's right for everyone, even if it isn't in your best interests." Maria tried to appeal to Bitsy's moral compass. But she should have known that was a shaky argument.

"Why?"

"Because if you don't, he's going to kill you," Maria said bluntly. "You know that. It's why you came to Adams-Larsen in the first place."

"He won't kill me," she said desperately. "I left a letter to be opened in the event of my death." But she didn't appear confident that she was safe. Maria couldn't count on Bitsy to save her.

Because she hadn't taken any precautions to protect Maria, their kidnappers likely considered Maria expendable.

Hadn't Bitsy said it yesterday? Maria didn't have anything to lose.

But as she contemplated her fellow prisoner, all she could think about was regret. That she hadn't appreciated Dwayne and she hadn't told him so. What if she had never met him?

She didn't believe in fate. Except if she hadn't been a captive for eight years, if she hadn't escaped and wandered into a retired marshal's yard, and he hadn't sent her to Jillian and Adams-Larsen, she and Dwayne might never have crossed paths. She would never have fallen for him.

She'd been lying to herself. Maybe she hadn't been expecting it but, she could admit now that she'd hoped for more than one night with Dwayne. Now she wished she'd pushed harder. She wasn't about to die a virgin.

Seize the moment.

"Is this what happened to you the last time?" Bitsy asked.

"I'm older now. I have skills. Training." She wasn't sure who she was trying to convince, herself or Bitsy. She hadn't fought. She'd cowered in the corner, just like Bitsy was doing now. "The last time my friends paid a terrible price."

"You won't…leave me behind?"

"Never."

"But—"

"I bleed for my friends, I grieve for their loss of innocence. And I made a promise to live a full productive life." That was why she forced herself to move across the country and take control. She wasn't about to let these assholes take her freedom.

Bitsy was still wavering. "I'm not brave enough."

"The second you make a deal with him he's going to demand that letter. You know that. And then he's going to kill you. That's pretty much a given." No way was Niles Vandenbeek letting her go. "The only way out is to fight."

Bitsy's shoulders slumped. "Okay. Yes." Then she straightened. "Do you have a plan?"

Maria outlined her idea. This had to work.

DWAYNE'S CELL RANG.

"We're going to get her back." Jill didn't even say hello.

"How?" Drive around in circles? Despair rolled through him.

"I tagged her rosary while she was at the salon the other day." Jill confessed. "We were able to pull up the signal and get you coordinates."

Dwayne and Jack were on the way.

Thank God Maria took that rosary with her everywhere. And thank God Jill had thought to tag it with a tracking device.

Maria would be pissed. But right now he didn't care as long as she was alive. All he wanted was to hold her in his arms. To tell her he was sorry. To convince her to take a chance on him.

Jack drove since he knew the area better than Dwayne. They headed up the mountain toward Truckee. The sky began to darken again. More snow was coming.

"I still can't figure out why Bitsy made that phone call." Kita had traced the call to Bitsy's stepfather. But even so, could her stepfather mobilize this fast?

The women had been missing for several hours. Vandenbeek had his own private plane. Based on when Bitsy had called her stepfather, he could be in Tahoe now.

But he didn't do his own dirty work. He had his head of security, Louis Gerber, do it. According to Jill's intel, Gerber was in DC at a security conference.

Dwayne tried to console himself with the thought that it would be difficult to organize something so quickly. Neither of the men in the surveillance tape was Bitsy's stepfather or Gerber.

"Let's just concentrate on getting them back," Jack said. "Clearly my worry about Maria was unfounded."

"What are you talking about?" But he knew.

"You have feelings for her." Jack pressed the accelerator down hard and the Range Rover shot up the inclined road. "You've got a pretty crazy reputation."

"I never hurt anyone, and they always knew my stance on relationships going in."

"But Maria is different."

Of course she was. Maria was unique. She was amazing. Dwayne's heart stopped when he considered she might already be dead. Not Maria.

But the truth was Niles Vandenbeek had shown no remorse for killing his mistress. Why would he give a fuck about Maria?

"I don't know what I'll do," he confessed. He couldn't bear the loss. She had to be okay. She had to be.

"We'll get there in time." Jack shot him a concerned look. "You gonna be solid?"

Dwayne took a deep breath. Fought for calm, froze his roiling emotions. There was no room for hysterics. What mattered was stone cold focus.

"I'm good."

They drove in silence, bypassing the town of Truckee and heading further up the mountain. The distance between houses grew. Most cabins were set back from the road and surrounded by pines and bushes to create privacy.

Global Positioning Systems in this area were notoriously inaccurate.

"Fuck."

"Our girl is resourceful. Don't panic."

Easy for Jack to say. His girl was safe.

SOMEONE WAS JIGGLING the shiny new lock on the bedroom door.

"This is it," Maria whispered. "You ready?"

"No," Bitsy whimpered.

"Suck it up." Maria stripped her robe off. She had ripped the thick expensive material to remove the robe from her body. That's where the hanger had come in useful.

Maria lay the robe next to Bitsy so it looked like she was huddled on the mattress. She headed for the open closet. "Remember the plan."

Bitsy lay on the mattress. She had the cowering part down pat. The massive guy who'd carried Bitsy stood in the doorway. He couldn't see Maria behind the door, but she recognized his voice when he growled, "Get up."

But Bitsy just lay there and cried.

This was the part they couldn't control. What if the other guy came in too? Maria hoped that the men didn't think two handcuffed women were a threat.

"Come on," he demanded. "He's on his way."

But Bitsy didn't move.

The guy snorted in disgust. "Stupid bitch." He strode over to the mattress. There was a small hitch in his step when he figured out that Maria wasn't in the robe but he'd already knelt down.

With a silent cry of rage, she jumped on his back, squeezing her legs around his ribs in a move Kita had shown her, looped her arms over his neck, and yanked the chain from the handcuffs tight against his thick neck.

The guy lurched to his feet and swung around, trying to dislodge her.

"Grab his gun," Maria commanded Bitsy.

The guy slammed her back against the wall. The contact

sang up her spine with brutal impact, but she didn't loosen her hold. If she couldn't choke him out, she was dead.

His breath wheezed as he curled his fingers around the chain.

He continued to pound her back against the wall. Shit. If she didn't neutralize him soon, the other guy would certainly hear them.

"Get. His. Gun." Each inhale like a sharp twist as he battered her against the wall.

Bitsy scrabbled for the gun but didn't have any luck.

Finally, finally the guy lost consciousness. He dropped to his knees and toppled forward. Maria was plastered over his back. Awkwardly, Maria extricated her arms from around the guy's neck, then scrambled from his body. She grabbed the belt from her robe and clumsily bound the guy's hands behind his back.

She shuddered. "Let's get out of here." Maria's breath heaved and her back was so sore, she hunched over like an old man.

Bitsy was sobbing. Snot and tears ran down her face and she hadn't grabbed the damn weapon.

She needed to cover up. Besides freezing, being naked made her feel vulnerable. "Come on," she hissed at Bitsy.

"What the fuck is taking so long?" The other guy stood in the doorway, gun in his hand.

Too late.

Chapter Seventeen

"Walk away," Maria said.

Bitsy stumbled to her feet, distracting him. While he wasn't looking at her, Maria grabbed the big guy's gun and aimed at the guy in the doorway.

He was so stunned he didn't move. Then he started laughing. "You think you can take me?"

Maria stood proudly, ignoring her nakedness even as he stared. Revulsion tossed her stomach, but her hand was steady. All those biweekly practice sessions at ALIAS's gun range were paying off. She wouldn't miss.

With a roar of rage, Bitsy rushed the man in the doorway, her arms up, her face a twisted mask.

"Get out of the way, you stupid bitch." He swung at Bitsy and Maria didn't have a good shot. She wasn't about to shoot their client.

"Leave her alone!" Bitsy yelled. The guy swung his arm in an arc and cuffed Bitsy on the head. She dropped to the floor.

Then he pointed his gun at Maria. He bared his teeth and leered at her. The wind howled outside the house, an echo of the cry in her soul. She shivered in the chill air when his gaze turned sexual.

"I thought you weren't supposed to hurt her?" Maria's teeth chattered, from cold, from fear.

"Can't kill her. Or hurt her." He revealed brown, tobacco-stained teeth. "You, however, are disposable. We were only supposed to grab *her*."

Her heart thudded so hard it banged against her ribcage. Her naked skin pebbled with goose bumps, from both the frigid air and the menace in his eyes.

"Before I kill you I'm going to fuck you."

Everything in her iced. She thought about how tenderly Dwayne had treated her, and she wished that he hadn't been so ready to stop her from losing her virginity.

"Put the gun down," he demanded.

Bitsy twitched.

"Not a chance in hell." Maria backed up, her arms steady as she aimed at the guy. She was so cold. So frozen.

She watched his eyes, never so thankful for those shooter drills in her life. "You don't have to be alive for me to fuck you," he growled.

His violent assertion brought back the memories, brought back Lucia's screams. Raped while Maria, Sophia and Graciela huddled in a corner, too terrified to do anything.

Not happening again.

He took a step toward her, and Maria pulled back the hammer on the unfamiliar weapon.

When he lifted his foot, Bitsy wrapped her hand around his ankle and yanked. The guy lost his balance and went down hard.

He fell backwards, his head hitting the wooden door jamb with a serious thunk.

Unfortunately, he pulled the trigger when he went down. The shot went wild and hit the ceiling. Plaster crumbled and hit the floor with little pings.

"Oh my Gawd." Bitsy scrambled away from him. "Is he dead?"

"Doubtful." Maria bent down and dug her hands, still cuffed, in the pocket of the first thug's jacket, searching for keys. To a car, to the cuffs. "We need to get out of here before they regain consciousness."

Bitsy was still staring at the guy on the ground. "I did it." The wonder in her voice was unmistakable. Her green eyes glittered, and joy spread over her face. "I did it!"

Maria found the car keys and held them up in triumph. "Yes!"

No keys to the handcuffs. But she could maneuver with them on. Then she grabbed the mutilated spa robe and shrugged into it. The robe hung awkwardly where she'd ripped it to get it off. "Let's go."

Maria thought about tying up the second guy but if they could get the hell out of here that wouldn't be necessary.

She tucked the weapon into the pocket of her robe. With quick efficient moves, she stripped the guy Bitsy had disabled of his weapon and handed it to Bitsy. "You know how to use one of these?"

Bitsy held the weapon between two fingers, every digit far away from the trigger. "I can figure it out." She was still riding high on her success.

"Okay, well put it in your pocket until we get to their vehicle."

Bitsy was in front of Maria as they raced down the hallway in search of an exit.

Bitsy skidded to a stop in the kitchen. Maria nearly ran into her.

An older man—with fair blond hair in a widow's peak, a hang of flesh under his chin, and crinkles around his malevolent smile—blocked their path. "Hello, *meisje*."

AFTER TWISTING and turning along the increasingly narrow road, Jack drove by the place where Maria's GPS signal was transmitting from. The small cabin looked deserted. The windows were shuttered and dark. The bear locker at the foot of the drive had a broken lock and one door hung crookedly. Overgrown brush hid the rest of the generally dilapidated house from view. A faded "For Sale" sign near the street was smudged with dirt.

The dirt-and-gravel driveway showed new tire tracks in the snow. Possibly more than one vehicle. Tall redwoods created a simple screen between properties, while allowing for a wide open feel.

Snow began to fall. The temperature had dropped and the sky darkened to an oppressive gray.

Jack parked in the driveway of the next cabin over. As they exited the car quietly, each checked their weapons. The steel was cold and ominous in Dwayne's hand. He had another weapon at his ankle and a knife in a sheath on his belt.

The surveillance tapes had shown Maria and Bitsy wearing spa robes. Hopefully they were in the cabin and not exposed to the elements.

Dwayne and Jack circled the rickety old cabin, creeping through the woods, weapons drawn searching for any opponents. A battered older model SUV and a shiny new Mercedes were pulled far into the gravel driveway almost behind the house.

Around the back of the cabin was a deck and an empty hot tub. Sliding doors led into the cabin. There were no lights on but Dwayne saw shadows behind the blinds that shielded the sliding doors.

The silence was absolute. The gentle snow fall should have been peaceful, but tension rode the back of his neck. Maria was in danger.

He wanted to rush in but that would be stupid. They needed to do surveillance first.

He prayed they weren't too late.

THE EVIL STEPFATHER. This was bad.

"Niles." Bitsy's voice quavered. Her face drained of color. Her gleeful pride had disappeared in a rush and her adrenaline high apparently morphed into fear with one word from Niles Vandenbeek.

A vivid memory struck out of nowhere. Her father had kissed her forehead and told her to have a good day the morning she'd been abducted. "*Te amo, mija.*"

She'd told him she loved him back. "*Te amo, papa.*" She'd danced around the kitchen like a goof, then headed for the bus stop to catch her ride to school.

At least she'd had warmth and affection for the first fifteen years of her life.

She'd had a loving relationship with her parents. Not always easy, but she'd known that they loved her. And she loved them.

As she stared at Bitsy's stepfather, she realized Bitsy had never had that support base. Contempt shone in Niles Vandenbeek's cold eyes.

Maria was behind Bitsy. Carefully, she slid her left hand

in the pocket of her robe. The cotton, soft and rich against her fingertips, contrasted with the deadly metal of the gun. Her heart thundered.

He appeared to be unarmed. Could she shoot someone who didn't have a weapon?

"What nonsense is this?" He spoke in a snooty upper-class manner with a hint of his accent. He didn't look dangerous. "You should not have brought someone else into our family squabble."

Maria snorted. His greed and criminal activities including soliciting murder were hardly a family disagreement.

"You are not going to get away with this!" Bitsy's voice rose.

They had to get out of here. Maria had the keys to the kidnappers' ride. They needed to flee before their kidnappers regained consciousness. They didn't have time for some big scene.

Bitsy's glow from her success had vanished.

They weren't going to get out of here until Bitsy got over her paralysis. Maria knew how important it was to face your attackers. Important and terrifying. But necessary.

"But of course I am." He brushed a piece of lint from the pocket on his shirt. "You're nothing but a pretty piece of ass who doesn't know when to shut up."

Bitsy curled in on herself, her shoulders hunching. Maria placed her right hand on Bitsy's shoulder, offering support. "You're smarter than this."

"Where are my men?" he demanded imperiously.

"You shouldn't be such a cheapskate, Niles," Bitsy said.

"We had to make do on the fly. But it doesn't matter." Niles Vandenbeek smirked. "I've got you right where I want you."

"No, you don't. I left a letter," Bitsy said defiantly.

"You're talking about the one on your computer?" He laughed, an annoyed bark of dismissal. His disdain obvious. "Already deleted from the cloud."

But Bitsy contradicted him. "You ass. I have copies in more than one place."

"I don't approve of vulgar language." He took a menacing step toward them.

"I don't fucking care." Bitsy had lost some of her fear. But she needed to hurry it up. If the guys in the bedroom woke up, their odds decreased dramatically.

"Bitsy, we need to get out of here."

"You're not going anywhere." His face turned red, and the smug look had disappeared as he narrowed his eyes. "Where is the information from my office?"

"It's too late for you." Bitsy straightened her shoulders. "I've already told people what they need to take you down."

"What people?" He took another step. "*Her?*"

"Among others."

He flung his hand toward Maria. "No one will miss some frumpy Latina woman."

"You don't read the papers enough, Niles."

Maria was Bitsy's ace in the hole? While she understood Bitsy's need to assert herself, Maria didn't appreciate being used.

"I have more power than your little friend."

"She's famous."

Niles rolled his eyes. "In your world, maybe."

Bitsy verbally jabbed at him again. "I'm going to testify against you."

"No one will believe you." Niles dismissed her claim. "You'll make a laughingstock of yourself and your mother. She'll never withstand the public scrutiny."

"That's where you'd be wrong."

"You write puff pieces for the *Washington Post* online." Niles flicked his hand. "You're conversant in fashion and makeup."

"You forget that I have a degree in journalism from Northwestern," Bitsy shot back. "You're done."

Maria was proud of her. "Nice job."

But they needed to get the hell out. Maria bared her teeth at the snake. "We'll be going now."

"Not so fast."

Bitsy shoved her hand into her pocket. "We're leaving." Her hand shook so badly that Maria was worried that she'd accidentally shoot herself or the jerk.

"Is that a gun?"

The poor girl's heart was beating so hard that her entire chest shook. But damn if Maria wasn't super proud of her. She'd stood up to her tormentor.

"You don't have the courage to shoot me." But Niles was pale, sweating, and the nervous tick at the corner of his eye gave him away.

Maria diverted the vile man's attention. "We can just leave. He isn't going to hurt us."

While Niles Vandenbeek was distracted, she eased her hand into her robe pocket and gripped the weapon with purpose. Bitsy might not shoot the guy but Maria had no compunction if he didn't let them leave. She was done with bullies and done with people who thought they could push around the less fortunate or the perceived weaker sex.

She'd never shot a person before but she was damn good with paper targets.

"You aren't going anywhere." His blue eyes blazed with fury. He was between them and the exit.

"I'm not just a pretty face," Bitsy said defiantly. "I can be and I will be more."

Before Maria could say another word, Bitsy pulled the trigger. Shot him.

Red blossomed on the arm of Vandenbeek's white dress shirt. Surprise and pain widened his eyes.

"You shot me!" Rage infused his face. He rushed them screaming, "Too bad you're a lousy shot."

But Maria wasn't. She whipped out her weapon and pulled the trigger.

Chapter Eighteen

A shot rang out.

Fuck waiting. Dwayne sprinted for the sliding doors.

"You're high. I'm low," Jack ordered. He didn't try and hold Dwayne back, for which he was grateful.

The slider was unlocked.

Pretty fucking bold. Unless there was no need for them to lock it.

Dwayne's heart nearly stopped.

Several shots echoed. Two different weapons.

They powered up the stairs, running toward the sounds.

"Maria," Dwayne roared.

He and Jack burst into the kitchen.

Niles Vandenbeek lay on the floor bleeding from several wounds and moaning.

Maria stood looking shell shocked, robe hanging off her shoulder, gaping open to show her naked body, and a weapon dangled from her cuffed hands.

"You're okay?" Dwayne strode in and scooped up Maria, cradling her to his chest. She moaned and arched away from his arm. "What's wrong?"

"Back," she groaned.

While Jack dealt with Bitsy, Dwayne turned her around. He slipped the robe away from her body so he could look at her back.

Huge bruises were forming all along her spine. "Oh, *la'u manamea*. What happened?"

He didn't want to touch her but when she began to shiver uncontrollably, he knew he had to get her covered up.

Her entire body shook but she lifted her bound wrists and bared her teeth in what passed for a smile. "Choked-out a guy. He objected."

Dwayne gently settled his coat around her shoulders. Her wince as the heavy down jacket touched her back slayed him but she needed to get warm.

"That's my girl." He lifted her arms to his mouth, wanted to weep at the angry red abrasions beneath the cuffs. "Where is he?"

Dwayne followed her down the hall to a bare bedroom. One man lay unconscious by the door, the other was attempting to lumber to his feet, hampered by his hands tied behind his back.

His knees nearly buckled when he took in the scene— bullet holes in the wall, plaster on the carpet, and the two men who'd abducted her and Bitsy—and how close she'd come to harm.

"Kita's training paid off," she said proudly.

"Damn straight." He'd have to give his pal Kita a giant smacking kiss on the mouth the next time he saw her.

Dwayne took care of the guy rolling around on the mattress first. He pulled some zip ties from his pocket and efficiently handcuffed the asshole. He may have pulled the plastic tighter than necessary.

He nudged the unconscious guy in the doorway. "What happened to him?"

"Bitsy took him down."

"Bitsy?" Their client?

"She did good," Maria said huskily.

"After she told the bastard where she was." His blood boiled. Bitsy had put Maria in harm's way.

Jack was on the phone calling the authorities. This was going to take a while.

Vandenbeek was moaning on the floor in the kitchen. Jack had used his belt to tourniquet the wound in his leg.

Dwayne gave in to the urge to touch her again. He wrapped his arms around her gently. She was safe. Everything in him relaxed, sighed in relief. "I'm glad you're okay."

"Yeah. Me too." Maria rested her forehead on his chest and curled into his warmth. He wanted to squeeze her tight and never let her go.

He wanted to apologize for running out. To confess that she'd hurt his feelings. But now wasn't the time or the place.

But all the things she'd said earlier came roaring back. She'd used him. Dwayne shut down his out-of-control emotions. "They didn't touch you?"

She shook her head and stepped back, as if she sensed his emotional retreat. "They didn't have a chance."

Thank God.

The warmth and relief he'd seen in her eyes when he'd put the coat around her shoulders was gone. A stoic woman in total control stood in her place.

"I'd appreciate it if you could see about keys for the cuffs."

Dwayne dug through the unconscious guy's pockets and

found the keys to the cuffs and released her. It appeared their truce was over.

———

MARIA SHOULD BE EXHAUSTED.

The events of the day kept playing on a continuous loop in her head.

She'd done it. She'd saved the client and herself.

She should be celebrating. She had kicked ass.

Instead she was lying on her stomach in the bed in the guest room, unable to quiet her mind.

Ever since the awkward moment in that ugly room in that horrible house, things between her and Dwayne had been strained.

Once Bitsy had come out of shock, she'd clung to Maria as if forgetting that she was the one who put them in danger.

As annoyed as Maria was, Bitsy was still their client.

Jack and Bliss were going to accompany them back to DC in the morning. Bitsy would be put into protective custody with the US Marshals. Her mother had already been picked up. They could have left tonight but Dwayne insisted that Maria needed to rest.

But resting wasn't working. She was anxious, wired, unsettled.

Someone knocked quietly on the door.

"Come on in." She figured it was Bliss checking up on her.

To her surprise, Dwayne walked in. "How are you feeling?"

"I've been better." The doctor had given her painkillers

for the severe bruising, but she didn't want to be impaired. She knew it was illogical but she needed to be ready to fight.

However once the adrenaline had worn off her back throbbed in pain.

She could sense him behind her, hovering. "Your poor back." His breath puffed against her neck. He was much closer than she'd expected.

Men. She wasn't sure she'd ever understand the male species. She definitely couldn't figure out Dwayne. He was back to being awkward around her.

"It will heal." So would her wrists. "Thank you for coming." *For me.*

"Of course," he said stiltedly. "Thank Jill for putting that tracking device in your rosary."

"I should probably be pissed."

"Maybe. But she knew you carried it everywhere."

"It's from my mother." The pain of loss made her voice tight. "She gave it to me…after."

"Oh. Well she'll be glad to know it saved you."

No, he had saved her. Actually she'd saved herself. "I haven't seen her. She mailed it to me."

"You haven't seen your mother since…."

"I was fifteen." She sighed, the sound full of exhaustion.

"I'll let you rest." He hesitated.

Dammit she didn't want him to leave. She was tempted to beg him to stay.

"He wanted to rape me," she blurted out.

"What!"

Yeah, she'd left that out of the official police report.

Dwayne sat down on the mattress next to where she lay. He brushed the hair away from her face so he could look into her eyes.

"No way was I letting that happen," she said fiercely.

"You're safe now." Heat rose between them, filled with his pine-scented deodorant and the slightly medicinal healing salve the doctor had put on her back.

She wanted to take back her power. Take back her confidence. Part of that was going after what she wanted. "Have sex with me."

"What?" Dwayne jumped to his feet.

"If you leave right now, I will never forgive you," she warned. "I want to have sex with you."

"But your back…."

Sensual feelings edged out the pain in her back. Longing. Need. Yearning.

"You're creative. We'll figure it out. And frankly, I don't care."

He bent and brushed a kiss against her forehead. "Why?"

"Because I was standing there naked, having that guy stare at me, and I knew that I'd lost an opportunity with you. I promised myself if I had the chance next time, I wouldn't settle for just playing."

"Oh, *la'u manamea*—"

"Don't." He was going to turn her down. Damn him. Maybe she deserved it, since he would likely assume she was using him.

That wasn't true.

She didn't just want a body. She wanted Dwayne. She totally got that she wouldn't be able to keep him. But she needed to take back her sexuality. And she wanted to do it with him.

DWAYNE STARED at the closed expression on her face, her body tense, her neck rigid. But not from physical pain. He'd hurt her without even trying.

How could he say no?

He trailed one finger over the curve of her ear, then bent to press a warm kiss against her cheek. "We'll have to be careful."

All the tension whooshed from her as his words sunk in. She buried her face in the pillow. "Not a problem."

The room was cast in a heated, sensual darkness, a single light glowing from the lamp on the dresser.

Dwayne lay down next to her. He slid his palm along her arm, his touch light as a feather, until he reached her fingers. He curled them in his and lifted her hand to his mouth.

Her breath caught when he pressed a heated kiss to her palm.

"Tell me if I hurt you."

The trust in her eyes slayed him. "Okay."

"You're sure?"

His cock had hardened, his muscles tensed. He would stop if she requested it, but he really hoped she still wanted him.

She pressed her palms against his shoulders and pushed until he lay on his back.

Then Maria straddled him and sat on his thighs. With deliberate movements, she unbuttoned her red flannel pajama top. Her nipples pushed against the fuzzy fabric. Her hair tumbled around her face, framing her soft cheeks and lush mouth.

While her movements were sure, her eyes were liquid and hesitant.

He caught her hands. "Let me."

She nodded. "'kay."

Maria stroked her palms along his forearms and then squeezed his biceps. "Love how strong you are," she whispered.

"You proved today that strength isn't everything." Smarts mattered. He spread her pajama top open, baring her breasts and silky skin.

The simple light created shadows on her body, and she flushed at his lazy perusal. "You are so fucking gorgeous." Her darkened nipples peaked, begging for his touch.

Dwayne smoothed his hands up the side of her ribcage, marveling at the softness of her skin. He cupped her breasts, holding their heavy weight in his hands, languidly strumming her nipples into tight peaks.

She moved with the rhythm of his fingers. Her sex heated as she rubbed against his growing erection, subtly trying to get him to move faster.

No way was he going to rush this.

He curled up. Maria reached for the hem of his T-shirt. She tugged the material over his head and tossed his shirt to the floor.

He traced her delicate collarbones with his fingertips, then he leaned in and pressed a single openmouthed kiss between her breasts. He tasted her skin in a sweep of kisses. "You're so soft."

Then he closed his mouth over her puckered nipple.

Maria clutched his head and pulled him closer. "And you're so hard."

He smiled against her breasts as he stroked her body in reverent touches. She responded with enthusiasm, tilting her head back, pushing her further into his voracious mouth.

He paused. "I want to eat you up." Then he suckled her harder, rolling her nipple on his tongue, savoring her surrender.

He learned her curves and relished her response as she returned his sensual exploration. Dwayne pushed his palm beneath the elastic waistband of her pajama bottoms, careful to avoid the bruises on her back.

He cupped her ass in his hands, her skin hot. She moaned as he eased her back and forth on his painfully hard cock.

The press of her mound was a pleasure pain he never thought he'd feel again. He'd been resigned to believing he'd never have another opportunity to touch her, thinking that she deserved a committed lover. Someone who would be there for her for more than a few nights.

But after today, he was following his own motto and seizing the day.

Dwayne pushed the flannel off her body so they were pressed against each other flesh to flesh.

He bumped her nose with his, and her lids lifted, her eyes hazy with pleasure.

Dwayne titled his head to the side and plundered her mouth. She opened so sweetly for him. Her tongue stroked his and she scored her nails along his scalp. Goose bumps raised at the sensual touch.

He wanted to hold on and never let her go.

Maria explored his body. Each caress increased his arousal, her hands sure and confident. His cock hardened. Blood rushed from his head, making him dizzy. He groaned against her, then ran his tongue along the cord of her neck.

Her nails dug into his shoulders.

She rocked harder against him. Her moans and sighs ramped him higher. "Oh," she sighed. Her thighs tightened against his legs.

He pushed his jeans-clad hips into the valley of her legs, keeping up the sensual assault.

She tried to lift, to reduce the pressure against her sex but Dwayne held her tight as she flew apart in his arms. A flush spread over her skin, lighting her up from the inside.

God, she was beautiful.

"Orgasm number one."

MARIA EXPLODED in a burst of light. Her sex contracted as her orgasm rolled through her in long hard pulls. Her bruised back forgotten, she frantically tugged at the button on his jeans. She didn't want him to change his mind. And she definitely didn't want to leave him hanging.

This afternoon when he'd come charging into that house, her first instinct had been to throw herself into his arms.

"I knew you'd come." Why she was thinking about this now, she had no idea. But she needed to let him know. "I knew it."

"I had complete faith in you." Dwayne elevated his hips, and with a superhuman lift of his arms, he held her aloft as he shoved the jeans down his thighs.

Maria got distracted by the flat disks of his nipples. She scored the small buds and he groaned. "Focus."

"I am." She smiled mischievously. "On you."

"Need your help. Don't want to hurt you." He couldn't get her pajama bottoms off. Maria pushed up into a down dog position, her hands by Dwayne's hips, her feet between his calves so he could remove the last barrier to her virginity.

Maria dropped her head and his erection was right in her face. "Well, this is interesting." The thick stalk jutted from the nest of black curls at the juncture of his thighs. A pulsing vein throbbed along his length, the engorged head almost purple. A pearly drop glistened on the tip. She dropped to her knees and bent to take him into her mouth.

She closed her eyes and delighted in the freedom to taste his salty musk.

She lavished him with sucking kisses and curled her tongue around his girth. His fingers slid through her hair and pulled her away gently. "Not this time."

Dwayne opened the drawer of the nightstand. He pulled out an unopened box of condoms and ripped the cardboard. Within seconds he tore open the foil package and rolled the latex over his erection.

She watched, fascinated. His big hands were rougher, not as careful as when she had handled him.

He paused. "You're sure?

Maria dropped her gaze to his cock. So big. She knew it would fit and still her breath hitched. She trembled with anticipation and a bit of fear.

"Yes." The moment she'd dreamed of, fantasized about, was finally here.

"I'll try not to hurt you." Dwayne trailed his fingers along her arms until he reached her hands. He threaded their fingers together.

Gently, he rubbed the head of his erection back and forth against her slick entrance. With each slide he penetrated her further. Her body had chilled and she felt exposed, open. For a moment, her vulnerability overwhelmed her.

But then she looked at Dwayne. He stared into her eyes, not looking away. This close the flecks of green and gold burned with an intense flame.

Dwayne anchored her with his gaze. Slowly, she sank onto his erection until she was filled to the hilt. Maria couldn't catch her breath. No pain, just an incredible fullness. As if the room had sucked all the air out, his body split hers in two, and yet connected them on another level. He was hers and she was his at this one perfect moment in time. Her channel clenched around him.

His cock pulsed against her walls in a slow, erotic rhythm. And still he didn't look away, acknowledging the weight of this moment. Her first time.

"You good?" His voice was soft, gentle in the hushed room.

He felt amazing. She felt amazing.

Her clit pressed down on his tight belly. Pressure built everywhere.

"It's lovely."

He raised his eyebrows and the spark that drew people to him appeared as he grinned. "Let's see if we can do better than *lovely*."

Dwayne released her hands. He cupped her neck in his large palm and encouraged her to come down over his chest. Her breast aligned with his mouth and he sucked her nipple. The answering tug deep inside was different when she was filled with him.

He commanded, "Straighten out. Lay on top of me."

Her heart hammered as he took control. She stretched her legs along the outside of his, the hair from his thighs scraping along her inner thigh. The unfamiliar sensation stimulated unexpected nerve endings. The position aligned their sexes, and Dwayne canted his hips up, moving in small slow thrusts.

Every movement rubbed her clit against his pubic bone, the tension doing amazing things to her body. Inside the pressure built again. His easy, smooth penetration drove against her inner walls. He rubbed another spot inside, and her body quivered on the brink of coming again.

The sense of connection swelled over her like a wave. Her hair fell around his face, curtaining them in a silent, sensual bubble.

They continued rocking against each other slow and easy until she needed to move. Maria rocked into him harder, faster.

Dwayne grunted, and when she stared into his eyes, she realized he was straining to go slowly. "Don't—" she gasped as he hit a particularly sensitive spot "—hold back."

Her permission unleashed his restraint, and Dwayne gripped her hips and pushed up inside her. Their easy contact transformed as new sensations bombarded her. She was being invaded and consumed with passion.

With every thrust she bounced on his flat stomach, the drag of her body over his hitting places she'd never imagined as erogenous. He banged into her, the head of his cock stimulating every nerve ending inside her.

And suddenly, Dwayne arched beneath her. His head thrown back, the tendons in his neck straining, she could feel his orgasm as he pulsed inside her. The force of his orgasm triggered her own.

Fireworks exploded. Sensation after sensation sparked and burst, filling up her empty places and freeing her as wonder spilled through her in a waterfall. She cried out in ecstasy.

Maria lay on top of him, her heart thundering, matching the rhythm of his heartbeat in her ear.

Sweat gleamed on his chest. As she came down from the incredible high, euphoria wound around her heart and spun in a lovely cocoon around them.

Before she could say a word, he brushed a kiss on her forehead. "Thank you."

He was thanking her? "For what?"

"Giving me the gift of your trust." There was a melancholy to his words.

He was still lodged inside her, binding her to him for this moment in time. But it wouldn't last. She knew that and still she held on.

She wanted so desperately to have him stay the night with her, but he shifted. "I need to take care of the condom."

And she knew their time together was done.

Dwayne extricated himself from her body and headed to the small bathroom attached to the guest bedroom.

Maria curled on her side, away from the door so she wouldn't have to watch him leave.

He returned from the bathroom and bent over the bed. With a gentleness at odds with his strength, he cleaned her sex, using tender care. "How's your back?"

It hurt like hell. "Fine." But she still would've liked his company in bed.

"Tomorrow is going to be a busy day." He hesitated, then brushed a barely there kiss on her hair. "Rest well."

Dwayne closed the door quietly. But then she swore she heard him whisper, "Be safe."

Chapter Nineteen

What did she do next?

She realized while they were guarding Bitsy and while she'd been kicking butt that she liked working in the field. She was pretty sure that no one had expected what happened in Tahoe, but she'd more than proven herself. She'd spent yesterday alone in her apartment going through the past week. Thinking about what she wanted next. She knew that it was time to move to the next level. She had always thought that when she was more grounded that she'd leave ALIAS, but she realized that she liked working there.

She loved her coworkers. Jill was an awesome boss. So much so that she called her and set the next phase of her life in motion.

"You're sure?" Jill asked.

"Positive."

"Okay. Be ready on Monday morning. I'll call the employment agency."

Now that her professional life was sorted, she needed to work on her personal life. Such as it was. Maria had achieved her biggest personal goal by having sex with

Dwayne. But with her limited knowledge, she hadn't factored in how much his rejection would hurt.

Somehow, she never envisioned past losing her virginity. Sure she'd had daydreams about a relationship but that was just a fantasy.

Naïve of her. But she was learning to navigate the messiness of living.

Dwayne's rejection would take time to get over.

But she realized that she'd based her expectations on an unrealistic fantasy that was never going to work for who she was.

Maria wasn't going to sit around and wait to be rescued. She handled things herself.

It was time to start making some decisions about what came next. To do that she had to be totally free of the past.

She thought about all those offers to tell her story. Thought about her friends. And knew what she had to do. Assuming people were still interested.

She made the call. "Hi. This is Maria Torres."

The excited squawking on the other end of the line cemented her decision. Editor Malika Jones calmed down. "Does this mean you're finally willing to give an interview?"

"I'll give you my story with conditions."

"This is fantastic news!"

Malika Jones's publication had a reputation for careful, well-researched articles that examined all sides of a controversial issue and treated the principals fairly. Frankly, Maria didn't care how she came across. And if her story helped one person, then it would be worth it.

Maria laid out her demands. They were willing to pay a crazy amount of money for her story. "One thing is non-negotiable." Maria said, "Half the money goes to the journalist of my choice. The other half needs to be sent directly to S.S.A.F.E."

"Who do you want to write the story?" Jones continued, "I have a list of our approved freelancers."

"I have a specific person in mind. I'll have her send you her resume. But she's who I want to write it." Of course, she hadn't asked yet. But she'd deal with that next.

"This is highly irregular." Jones hesitated. "But okay. We can always tweak the content and language if needed."

"Any changes have to be approved by the journalist who writes the article."

"Are you sure you want the journalist to get half? That's awfully…generous." Jones tried to counsel Maria.

Maria glanced around her tiny apartment. The most expensive thing she owned was her television. She didn't care about things. This was the right thing to do. "Yes."

They haggled over some final details, but Maria had gotten what she wanted. "Email me the contract and I'll sign it and send it back to you."

She hung up the phone.

Next up. She needed to contact the right journalist.

But she didn't have her phone number, so she went downstairs and flagged a taxi.

MARIA'S HEART pounded as the taxi pulled up in front of the typical suburban house. The driveway was littered with cars. It occurred to her that it was Sunday. She been impulsive. A character trait she rarely indulged and had tried to stamp out. It was tempting to turn around and go home.

Instead she paid the cab driver and exited the taxi.

She scanned the vehicles but didn't see Dwayne's car. Maria took a deep breath and blew it out. Thank goodness.

She knew she'd have to face him again in the office. But right now she was thankful for the reprieve.

Hesitantly she rang the doorbell.

She could hear chatter coming from inside the house, and someone yelling, "I'll get it."

The door swung open. A gorgeous woman, petite and rounded, said, "Can I help you?"

"Ah, yes, hi." Maria shifted nervously from foot to foot.

"Who is it?" Dwayne's mother peered around the woman's shoulder. "Maria! Come in, come in."

"Who is this, mama?" She eyed Maria suspiciously.

"Talia, where are your manners?" She slapped Talia gently on the arm. "This is Maria from Tupua's office."

Talia. The teacher.

"Nice to meet you," Maria said softly. "Thank you, Mrs. Lameko."

"Didn't I tell you to call me Mama?"

Maria flushed.

"Come in and meet my daughters."

All of them?

Uh oh. This was definitely not what she had planned. "Oh, uh, that isn't necessary. I was just wondering if I could get Samaria's phone number."

"You don't need her number. You can come in and talk to her now."

"I don't want to intrude."

"Nonsense." She pulled Maria into the house.

Inside the noise level increased exponentially, but when she walked into the kitchen, all the conversation stopped.

Maria felt like an oddity on display as the group of beautiful women stared at her. "This is Maria. From

Tupua's office." His mother introduced her with a flourish of her arm.

"Hi," Maria said awkwardly.

"These are the twins. La'ei."

The fashion addict.

"And Lulu."

The accounting major.

"Sefina."

The lawyer.

"Natia."

Med school.

"And here is Samaria."

The journalist. And just who she needed to speak with.

"Where's Teuila?"

"*Of course*, everyone knows T." La'ei griped, just as Lulu replied, "On a shoot."

"Ah, well, it's nice to meet you all." Maria smiled shyly, overcome by the sheer beauty of Dwayne's family.

Mama patted Maria on the shoulder. "You want to come to church with us?"

"No thank you." Maria fingered the rosary beads in her pocket. "Um, could I have a word with Samaria? Then I'll go. I didn't mean to interrupt your family day."

She did wonder where Dwayne was. But she was definitely thankful that he wasn't here right now. That would have been awkward.

"You are welcome any time." Dwayne's mother shooed the rest of the women into the family room next to the kitchen.

Samaria looked confused but led her into a small office off the entry. "What can I do for you?"

"How would you feel about writing a feature article?"

Samaria's mouth dropped open. "About you?"

Maria nodded, her hands clasped together at her waist. "You probably want someone with more experience."

Her hopes fell. She had just assumed that Samaria would say yes. "You don't want to do it?"

Samaria bounced on her toes. "Are you kidding me? Of course I want to. I'd kill to do your story. But…why me?"

"Because I know your brother. He has so much integrity and he speaks so highly of you."

"So you're doing this for Dwayne?"

And his family. With three sisters still in college, they all pitched in. Maria knew the money would be well spent.

"I negotiated with the magazine." She named the fee Samaria would get and Dwayne's sister leaned against the wall as if her legs didn't work.

"Oh my God!" Samaria threw her arms around Maria. "Thank you."

Maria only fidgeted a little as Samaria hugged her.

"When do we start?"

"Whenever you want." Maria hesitated. "Although the editor said if it was submitted by Tuesday, they could bump something to get it in next month's issue."

"We can't do the interview here." Samaria said, "I give it another five minutes and mama will interrupt us to see if you want something to eat. How about your place?"

An hour later, they were back at Maria's apartment. Mrs. Lameko had indeed fed Maria and the sisters a snack.

Maria felt bad about pulling Samaria away from church, but she had insisted.

They decided to go to Maria's apartment for the interview. After circling the block a few times, Samaria found a parking spot on the street near Maria's apartment and they walked the two blocks.

Samaria kept up a steady stream of chatter, so Maria

didn't need to say much. She was as charming as her brother with a quick smile and an easy manner.

Samaria set up her recorder at Maria's tiny bistro table. "Are you ready?"

Her palms were clammy and her heart rate had picked up.

"We can always do this another time," Samaria said gently.

"No. The only way to move forward is to get this out and move on."

"Okay. Since I didn't prepare for this, I'm going to just let you tell your story in your own words." Samaria patted the steno pad in front of her. "I'll make notes as you go and then I'll ask questions."

"Let's do it."

And Maria began her story, reliving the kidnapping, Lucia's rape, years in the basement, her escape, and the harrowing and difficult journey to adjust to living around people again.

Samaria asked thoughtful and thought-provoking questions, getting Maria to open up even further. Every time she thought about holding back, she remembered Sophia and Graciela.

Maria had been given a gift. She was alive, and free, and working toward happiness. She was duty bound to share her ordeal so she could help her friends who had not been as fortunate.

Samaria's eyes were wet when they finished. Maria was wrung out. She hadn't cried, even though reliving those eight years and then her life after it was emotionally draining.

She could hear neighbors talking loudly in the hallway, but she ignored them.

"I can see why my brother admires you."

Maria jolted. "What?"

"He talks about you a lot."

"Me?" That couldn't be right.

"Sure. At our Sunday dinners, he constantly mentions you. Maria achieved this. Maria did that."

"I'm so confused." The man who practically ran away from her for a year talked about her to his family?

"For awhile I thought that maybe he and you…."

Maria didn't know what to say. "Not until this past week."

"Oh. Oh! That's great!"

"He doesn't want me," Maria said.

He said he didn't want more responsibility. Didn't he? Except she had said that having sex with him was convenient because of his reputation. She'd lied to protect herself. He'd been perfect because of who he was. A caretaker.

She hadn't just been using him. And she had never told him that. "I may have screwed up."

A knock at the door interrupted her revelations. "Gas company."

"Excuse me." Maria got up to answer the door. She stared out the peephole but all she could see was the top of a cap that had the gas company logo on it.

She opened the door. "Can I help you?"

"Gas leak in the building. We need everyone out." The man lifted his head and smiled. His white face and blue eyes looked familiar. Then his eyes widened. "Hello, Maria."

How did the gas company employee know her name? Then she realized why he looked familiar.

Louis Gerber.

They had seriously miscalculated.

Chapter Twenty

Dwayne walked in the door of his family home needing the touchstone to comfort him. Except as he stood in the foyer, he remembered the last time he'd been here. His mother had hugged Maria and she'd been stiff in the embrace.

Everything reminded him of Maria.

He had wanted to stay in that bed and sleep with her, hold her and be grateful she was alive. But, she'd just been using him. She asked and he delivered. But his heart couldn't take any more. He had feelings for her. And another rejection would crush him.

But dammit, walking away from Maria had gutted him.

Fortunately, work had taken his mind of everything for the past few days. ALIAS had been dealing with getting Bitsy and her mother into witness protection through the US Marshals office and constructing a case against Vandenbeek once Bitsy had given her official statement. Niles Vandenbeek was being sent back to DC after he was processed for kidnapping and attempted murder in California. There were still plenty of prosecutorial obstacles that had to be surmounted and right now the authorities were looking for Louis Gerber. He was a loose end in the case. There was an arrest warrant issued but so far Vandenbeek's head of security was nowhere to be found.

"Tupua!"

His sisters gathered around him, giving him hugs. He loved his family. He was so grateful for their support. He thought about Maria and how she had no one.

"We met Maria!" His sisters shouted, as if he conjured her just by thinking about her.

What? He nearly stumbled. "Where?"

"She came to see your sister," his mother said.

He scanned their faces. Teuila and Samaria were missing. "Which one?"

"Samaria."

Before he could ask why, his phone buzzed in his pocket. "I'm waiting on some news, so I need to take this." He pulled out his phone, hoping for a positive update from the police.

Instead, he had a text from Samaria. "S.O.S."

Then a picture came through.

His heart stopped.

MARIA BLOCKED THE DOORWAY.

"There's a gas leak?" She tried to play it off. She needed to get Samaria out of here. Her one thought was to protect Dwayne's sister. Then she could go about saving herself.

Gerber shoved into her apartment and saw a wide-eyed Samaria at the bistro table.

"Who is she?" he snarled.

"You should go. Apparently there's a gas leak," Maria

said in a perky voice, desperately trying to message Samaria with her eyes to get the hell out.

"I don't want to leave you." Samaria was visibly shaking.

"It's all good. You go ahead." She gestured Samaria toward the door. "I just need to grab…." Maria frantically tried to come up with something that would cause her to stay behind, but her mind was blank.

"Shit." Gerber pulled out a gun. "No one goes anywhere."

Samaria squeaked.

"I'm sure we can work this out, Mr. Gerber."

She realized her mistake immediately. She should never have given away that she knew who he was. She quickly tried to distract him. "How did you find me?"

"I'm in security, you idiot."

It made no sense to pretend ignorance. "How did you know who I was?"

"The men I hired in California sent pictures of you and your pal, Bitsy, as proof of life."

He thought she and Bitsy were friends. So maybe he didn't know she worked for ALIAS. She'd take any advantage she could get. Gather information, build a picture, and put a plan together, just like Dwayne said.

"Your boss is in jail in California."

"I know that." He paced her studio apartment. Maria kept one eye on his weapon. It was big, probably a 9 mm. In her small space it could do a lot of damage.

She asked a few more questions, but he didn't answer any of them. Time to prod him.

"You should probably be trying to leave the country since you killed Niles Vandenbeek's mistress."

Samaria's brown eyes widened even further.

"Shut up." He gestured to the tiny love seat with the weapon. "Both of you sit down over there."

"Where is Bitsy?" he demanded.

She had no clue where Bitsy was. The marshals had taken her away. Maria's job right now was to get Samaria away from this guy.

"Not telling."

"What were you doing in California?"

"Hiding from Vandenbeek."

"You were hiding her?" He looked her up and down derisively.

"I was doing her a favor."

She couldn't let him know she worked for a company that protected people. He might decide she was expendable.

"That trip took money. And clearly you don't have any." Gerber sneered. "Who do you work for?"

Nope. Not giving up ALIAS.

Maria simpered. "Why don't we just let my friend go and then I'll be happy to help you."

"Fuck you."

"Fine." Playing the idiot wasn't getting her anywhere. "You hurt her, and you won't get a thing from me," Maria said fiercely.

"Give me what I want. Tell me where Bitsy is and I'll let you both go."

But Maria knew he had no intention of letting them go. He'd killed Vandenbeek's mistress. He'd have no compunction about killing her or Samaria. Her only recourse was to help Samaria get away. And then try to disable him. Too bad he was built like a tank. "Why do you want Bitsy?"

"She has something of mine."

Bitsy said she'd overheard them. Not that she had

physical evidence against Gerber. Of course, anything was possible.

"I can't tell you where Bitsy is."

He aimed his weapon at Samaria.

"*Dios mío*, no! She's with the US Marshals." Maria flung her arms wide to make herself more of a target and protect Samaria. "I literally don't know where she is."

"God dammit." He punched the television with his left fist. The LCD screen shattered, raining slivers all over the floor.

She needed to misdirect him. "But I can tell you when they are taking her to the courthouse."

He growled. "Not enough."

"And…I know where she hid the evidence she took from her stepfather's study."

Total lie. But if she could get him away from Samaria it would be a win. She had no intention of dying but she also needed to protect Dwayne's sister.

"I promise."

He studied her. "Okay. Let's go."

There was a commotion in the hallway. "What's all that noise?"

"Didn't you hear? There's a gas leak in the building."

"You engineered that?"

"I traced you to this building through facial recognition technology and the government cameras on the street. But I didn't know which apartment was yours, so I went door to door."

Even though she didn't take ALIAS up on the relocation they'd taken steps to hide her from the press. This apartment was actually in Jill's name. They hadn't accounted for someone hacking into the CCTVs. But that helped her plan. If she could get them outside Samaria could run.

He wouldn't dare shoot in a crowd.

"Let's go."

Maria held out her hand to Samaria, who was shaking hard. "It'll be okay."

Samaria whimpered and Maria wrapped her arm around her shoulders and squeezed tight. She fingered the rosary beads in her pocket and prayed to a God she no longer believed in. *Please don't take Dwayne's sister away from him.*

"Give your brother my love."

It was the closest she could come to telling Samaria to tell Dwayne that she loved him. Because dammit she did. It was funny how clarity came while facing the wrong end of a pistol.

DWAYNE RACED to Maria's apartment building.

He'd called ALIAS and Jill, Kita, Jake and Viktor were on their way. But he was the closest.

A crowd had gathered on the sidewalk outside. "What's happening?" he asked a guy in sweats holding a cat carrier.

"They said there was a gas leak." He glanced around and frowned. "But where's the gas department?"

Dwayne rushed inside and up the stairs. Tenants were still pouring out of the building. He had to battle the flow of people on the stairs going in the opposite direction.

Be safe. His last words to her—the same his mother gave before he got on an airplane—had been spoken through the door, and he had no idea if she'd even heard them. He wondered, even if she had heard him, would she understand what those words really meant?

He burst out of the stairwell and into the hallway on the fourth floor.

His sister was walking jerkily toward the elevator with Maria behind her, shielding her from the guy in the uniform and ball cap. The way Maria was walking, Gerber must have a gun on her.

For a moment, he froze.

This was his worst nightmare. One of his family in danger. Maria in danger.

And he'd let her go. Pushed her away because he was an idiot.

She had to survive. She'd been kidnapped twice and escaped both times. This was not going to be her downfall.

Dwayne barreled toward the trio, unholstering his weapon as he ran headlong down the hallway.

Maria's eyes opened wide and she gave a small shake of her head. She fingered something in her pocket.

But it was too late. Gerber had seen him.

Maria shoved Samaria. His sister fell to the ground as Maria whipped around and swung her rosary beads into Gerber's eyes. He hadn't seen it coming because he'd been focused on Dwayne.

He cried out, "You bitch."

And then with a primal yell, Maria followed up with a roundhouse kick to the guy's temple. She must have hit him just right, because Gerber went down like a brick.

Dwayne got there just in time to put his knee in Gerber's back. Fortunately he still had some zip ties in his pocket and he quickly restrained Gerber.

Adrenaline coursed through his body as he thought about what could have happened.

Samaria sat up on the floor and smiled at him woozily. "Your crush is a badass." And then she fainted.

Maria caught her before her head hit the floor.

"Good timing," she panted as she held his sister in her arms. The elevator dinged.

"Maria, I—"

Kita burst through the barely open elevator doors. "Man, I missed all the fun."

"Looks like you have everything in hand." Jill followed along with Viktor and Jake.

"Let me take a look at your sister." Viktor carried Samaria into Maria's apartment.

The rest of the crew piled in. And the moment was lost.

Chapter Twenty-One

Dwayne waited impatiently for everyone to leave.

Maria sat at the bistro table in her tiny apartment answering Jill's questions. The single room studio was not designed for all these large people.

Gerber was finally gone. The FBI had taken him to the local jail to be processed.

Viktor and Jake had taken Samaria home after she'd been questioned.

Kita sat at the table with Maria who still looked like she was on a high from once again kicking ass.

What stuck out was her confident smile as she spoke with Jill. Her lips were stained with a bright coral that matched the flecks in her sweater.

He'd suffered through the past few hours, waiting for everyone to leave. He couldn't wait another minute. "Can I talk to you?"

"Oh, hi." She didn't look away.

Less than a week ago she would have blushed and averted her gaze, but now she confronted him boldly. He loved the change in her.

Kita glanced between the two of them. "Jillian. I do believe it's time for us to head out."

"Thanks, Kita." Dwayne smiled.

"Don't thank me yet." Kita slapped him on the shoulder.

Jill said, "Don't forget I need you at the office around nine tomorrow. The first applicants should arrive around ten."

"I'll be there in time to help with the interviews." Maria wrapped her cardigan around her shoulders and stood.

"See you tomorrow." Jill and Kita waved.

Dwayne watched everyone go. "Applicants?"

"For the receptionist job." Her eyebrows quirked.

His brain stalled. She was leaving? "Where are you going?"

Maria tilted her head, her black hair falling over one shoulder. "I'm going to start training for the field."

"What? No!"

"What do you mean no?"

"I mean absolutely not."

She narrowed her gaze. "You don't get a say in what I do."

"I'll talk to Jill." He couldn't stand it if something happened to her.

"I did a great job in Tahoe," she shot back. "And with Gerber."

"You did." He may have nearly had a heart attack. Both times. But she'd held her own.

"Then what the hell is your problem?" She stalked into his personal space and bumped right up against his chest.

The softness of her breasts, the scent from her hair, and the fiery sparks shooting from her eyes, he'd wanted them all.

"I don't want anything to happen to you." He couldn't stand it any longer. He crowded her against the kitchen counter and wrapped his arms around her shoulders. "Don't you get it?"

Her voice was muffled against his neck. "Why?"

"You matter."

She felt so good pressed against him. "Well that's nice and all, but I like being in the field. I like the adrenaline. I like making a difference."

The thought of her being out there where he couldn't keep her safe made him crazy. His arms tightened around her, but he didn't say anything because he listened to what was underneath her words. The job gave her life meaning. Wasn't that the same reason he did what he did?

"You want me to just sit back and not live up to my potential?"

"No." He sighed. "But I nearly lost it when we couldn't find you and when Gerber had you."

She pushed away from him. "But you didn't."

"There was no time to fall apart," Dwayne confessed. "Failure was not an option."

"So then protect me."

Dwayne thought about her suggestion. "It could work."

"Of course it will work."

"Are you sure you trust me?" Dwayne needed to know. "I didn't swoop in and save you. I wasn't your prince."

"I was fifteen when I had that fantasy. I don't need a prince. I need a partner."

A partner. Someone else to depend on him.

Except that Maria didn't just depend on him, she also supported him. They could share their burdens and their triumphs.

"I already talked to Jill," she said quickly. She pressed

her hand to his chest right over his heart. "We make a good team."

They did.

Maria's palm trembled with every thud of his heart against her touch. "ALIAS doesn't have any rules against fraternization. So we could be partners."

"True." Dwayne needed to know what she was suggesting. He should have figured out that she'd go after what she wanted. His angel was full of courage.

"Just partners at work?" she pushed.

"Not good enough." Revealing the rest was hard but he pushed the words out. "I want…you."

"That's good because I want you too."

Then he voiced what had been worrying him the most. "But you've never dated anyone else."

MARIA STARED into Dwayne's dark, somber eyes. The hurt pressed down on her chest, made it difficult to breathe. "You want me to date other men?"

"Fuck, no."

"Well then why would you suggest it?"

"I just don't want you to have regrets."

"The only thing I regret right now is telling you I want you." Her comeback was sassy.

He wrapped his big biceps around her and lifted her on to the countertop, just like he had in the kitchen at the cabin. Way too gently.

"I'm not fragile, you know."

"I don't want to hurt you."

"You won't." They definitely still had some things to work out but that could be dealt with later. He wanted her.

For now, it was enough.
"What if—"
"Shut up and kiss me."
So he did.

Epilogue

They pulled up to the office in Dwayne's compact car. Maria ran her hand over the steering wheel and gave Dwayne a chance to peel his fingers from the roll bar on the passenger side.

She was learning to drive but was harrowing.

"I never asked you. Why this car?" It was really small for someone his size.

"Best safety rating." Dwayne smiled at her. "And my mother asked me to."

"I love how much you love your mother." Maria smoothed her hand over her wool skirt. "Although spending Thanksgiving with your family is going to be intimidating."

"Not as intimidating as meeting your mother."

Her heart expanded. Dwayne had gone with her to see her mama. Unfortunately her mother's dementia had deteriorated. For one glorious hour, she'd known who Maria was and then she'd descended back into a time when Maria hadn't been kidnapped. Hadn't disappeared. She could hardly be disappointed if her mother's disease erased that horrible time.

Maria remembered for both of them.

She fingered the rosary in her pocket. She leaned across the console and pressed her lips to his.

He closed his hand over her fist. "You'll be great."

While Samaria, Sefina and Teuila were on board with their relationship, his younger sisters were a harder sell. "Easy for you to say. You're their revered older brother."

"But my mother loves you."

Mrs. Lameko had taken Maria under her wing. She hadn't just found her new normal, she'd found a family too.

She was in love with Dwayne. But she hadn't quite gotten up the nerve to tell him so. She'd sort of been waiting for him to go first.

They were at the office early this morning because Maria had her first assignment.

After a quick team meeting, Maria headed out to pick up their client. She would be escorting Bitsy to the court for a Grand Jury hearing on Van Pharmaceuticals and her stepfather's shifty illegal practices.

Nile Vandenbeek was in jail without bond because he'd been deemed a flight risk due to dual citizenship and his Swiss passport. Louis Gerber was also in jail.

Turned out the files Bitsy had stolen were seriously incriminating. Between the files and his arrest in Tahoe, Niles Vandenbeek wasn't just in trouble with the House committee. He was going to prison for a long time.

Thrill and excitement competed for dibs on her mood. But that he was here, supporting her, believing in her was the biggest thrill of all.

"Be safe."

She knew it meant I love you. But one day it would be nice to hear the words.

I love you, she mentally added. "I will. I've got Jake as

driver and backup." The team was listening in. Everyone's comm devices were tuned to the same channel.

She started to get in the bulletproof Range Rover. Not that Bitsy was in imminent danger but they weren't taking any chances.

"Wait." He grabbed her, lifted her off her feet until their mouths were level. He kissed her hard.

Now Maria flushed because everyone was listening and Jake was watching avidly.

"*Oute alofa ia oe*," he said fiercely.

"What does that mean?" But she had a feeling she knew.

"I love you."

Her heart exploded with joy, beating at warp speed as she wrapped her arms around his neck.

"Aww, isn't this sweet?" Kita's voice echoed in her ear.

Dwayne could hear her too. "Fuck off, Kita."

Hardly the tender declaration of love that accompanied most first times. But when had Maria ever done anything the standard way?

Her whole life had been extreme, and unusual, and that wasn't about to change. So with everyone listening, she said, "I love you too."

THANK YOU, thank you for waiting patiently for Maria's story. I hope you loved Maria and Dwayne as much as I did. If you did enjoy this novel, below are a few ways you can help a writer out!!

GOOD: Lend the book to a friend

· · ·

BETTER: Recommend the book to your friends

BEST: Leave a review at Amazon, BN, iBooks, Kobo, Google Play, Goodreads...basically any place they sell or review eBooks. Every review helps my work get out to other readers and I cannot even express how much it means to me when you let people know you liked my work. Readers have so many choices nowadays and limited dollars to spend. It can be difficult to take a chance on a new author even if the premise sounds appealing. By reviewing books, you give other readers insight into the story world and help them make informed purchases.

THANK YOU, thank you, thank you for your support!!

P.S. Want to know how the whole saga surrounding Maria started? Stone Cold Heart, the first book in the Family Stone series, is FREE on all retailers.

p.p.s. Want to read about how Kita found her Fed? Read Stalked the first book in the ALIAS series.

p.p.p.s. Would you like to know when my next book is available? You can sign up for my new release email list/newsletter at Lisa's Confidants I send out newsletters once a month typically filled with info on upcoming books, friend freebies, and contests I'm involved in. I will never sell or distribute your email to other people.

Also by Lisa Hughey

Black Cipher Files Romantic Suspense

The Encounter, A Prequel to Blowback

Blowback

Betrayals

Burned

Dangerous Game

Black Cipher Files Box Set (includes Blowback, Betrayals, and Burned)

Snow Creek Christmas

Love on Main Street: A Snow Creek Christmas – 7 Author anthology

One Silent Night (from Love on Main Street)

Miracle on Main Street (standalone novella)

Family Stone Romantic Suspense

Stone Cold Heart, (Jess, Family Stone #1)

Carved in Stone (Connor, Family Stone #2)

Heart of Stone (Riley, Family Stone #3)

Still the One (Jack, Family Stone #4)

Jar of Hearts (Keisha & Shane, Family Stone #5)

Queen of Hearts (Shelley, Family Stone #6)

Cold as Stone (John, Family Stone #7)

<u>Family Stone Box Set (Stone Cold Heart, Carved in Stone, Heart of Stone, Still the One, & Jar of Hearts)</u>

<u>The Nostradamus Prophecies</u>
<u>View To A Kill #1</u>
Never Say Never #2

<u>ALIAS</u>
Stalked (ALIAS #1)
Hunted (ALIAS #2)
Vanished (ALIAS #3)
Saved (ALIAS #3.5)
Deceived (ALIAS #4)

<u>Billionaire Breakfast Club</u>
His Semi-Charmed Life (Billionaire Breakfast Club #1)
Everything He Wants (Billionaire Breakfast Club #2)
Queen of His Daydreams (Billionaire Breakfast Club #2.5)

About Lisa

USA Today Bestselling Author Lisa Hughey started writing romance in the fourth grade. That particular story involved a prince and an engagement. Now, she writes about strong heroines who are perfectly capable of rescuing themselves and the heroes who love both their strength and their vulnerability. She pens romances of all types—suspense, paranormal, and contemporary—but at their heart, all her books celebrate the power of love.

She lives in Cape Ann Massachusetts with her fabulously supportive husband and one somewhat grumpy cat.

Beach walks, hiking, and traveling are her favorite ways to pass the time when she isn't plotting new ways to get her characters to fall in love.

Lisa loves to hear from readers and has tons of places you can connect with her. It's a wonder she gets any writing done at all….

Be Lisa's Friend on Facebook
Sign Up for Lisa's Confidants
Visit Lisa on the Web

Follow Lisa on Pinterest
Follow Lisa on Instagram
Email Lisa
Be Lisa's Friend on Goodreads
Like Lisa on Facebook at Lisa Hughey Author